JOSHUA AND THE MAGICAL FOREST

Christopher D. Morgan

Portallas - Book 1

portallas.com

This novel has been written using British English spelling and conventions.

This book was previously published under the name
Forestium: The Mirror Never Lies
Although the title has changed, the content has not.

Joshua and the Magical Forest is book 1 in the Portallas series.

Fifth edition (First published March 2016)

Edited by Gordon Long
Cover design by Christian Bentulan
Illustrations by Stepan Bybyk
Stock images from ybsilon-stock.deviantart.com

59,397 words.

ISBN-13 (hardback):
978-0-9945257-1-0

ISBN-13 (paperback):
978-0-9945257-0-3

ISBN-13 (e-book):
978-0-9945257-2-7

For Patsy.

FORESTIUM

MORELLE

SOUTHERN
TIP

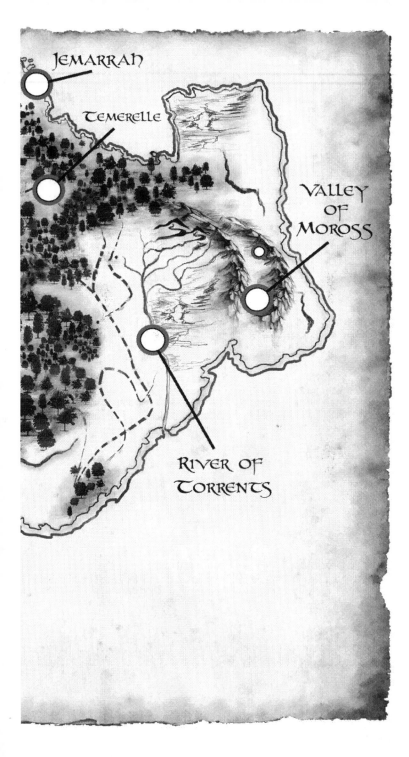

Prologue

Melachor and Veloria stopped just long enough to catch their breath.

Melachor felt Sandor's forehead with his palm. The skin was still damp and hot to the touch. The infant's breathing had become increasingly laboured and he was now gasping for breath. Melachor stared at the tattered map, his hand shaking.

"Please, Melachor, we must rest." Veloria leaned against a grungy building, barely able to stand, with the infant limp in her arms. Her fatigued toddler whined as he clung to her.

Sandor continued whimpering. Time was running out. Melachor shook his head and heaved a sigh as he caught his wife's eye. She clutched a protective arm around Jared's shoulders. Both of them feared their toddler might also catch this plague.

They peeked up and down the filthy alleyway. Screams rang out from all directions. Pandemonium in the distance wrenched at their attention but Sandor's wellbeing was all they could focus on right now.

"This way, Vel," he said, leading his exhausted family further into the maze of backstreets.

People had been running for cover, and the winding alleys were now all but empty. The sun's rays didn't penetrate into these narrow passages and a foul stench hung in the air. Shady figures lingered in the shadows, and he felt eyes staring at them from hidden corners.

The rickety, wooden buildings gave no outward sign of what lay behind each door. Melachor knew it was unsafe to bring his family here, but if Sandor were to stand any chance of surviving the illness, he needed to find a Metamorph, and quickly. The pox had claimed so many lives already and time was running out for Sandor.

Although no longer a Trader, Melachor had spent many years travelling from village to village and was a good listener. It was by no means clear whether the legends were true or just tales told by drunks and con artists. But these were desperate times. The map was the only clue they had to help them find the mythical creature, and it had led them to these backstreets. Melachor had risked his life to get his hands on the map and he hoped it was not in vain.

Veloria clutched Sandor in one hand and clung to Jared with the other. She shuffled closely behind her husband as he led them through the muddy alleys.

The family reached an intersection. Melachor looked in all directions, trying to find a familiar landmark, but his search was in vain. It had been too long since he was last here in the Southern Tip. Already one of Forestium's largest settlements, it had grown considerably in recent years.

"Melachor, are you sure we're doing the right thing? It isn't safe. We're never going to find one here. The trader that gave you the feather could have been lying."

More screams from terrified Imps rang out in the distance. Melachor, too, feared for his family's safety. A storm was brewing and they could hear thunder rumbling in the distance.

They looked up at the dark clouds stealing what little daylight they could still see.

"Look," he said, "it makes sense that there would be a Metamorph here. If there are any left, this is where they'll be and this is exactly where the map says we'll find one. It's easy to hide here. I've been a trader for a long time and I know when to spot a lie. Just don't lose that Raetheon feather."

Veloria pulled out the white tail feather and showed it to her husband. Before she could tuck it away, a short, plump Imp wearing a pointed hat and scruffy, brown waistcoat emerged from the mist in one of the dark alleyways.

"Looking for something, are we? Dangerous place to be wandering around with children, if you don't mind me saying. Not safe for anyone to be outside right now."

Melachor looked down at the Imp and narrowed his eyes. Clutching at his wife's hand, he opened his mouth to speak, but hesitated. The man stared at him, but remained silent.

Melachor felt he was out of options. He had reached the point that he needed to take the risk.

"I'm looking," he whispered, "I'm looking for a Metamorph."

The man squinted up at Melachor and glanced at the sickly child its mother clutched to her chest.

"I don't know what you mean," the Imp said dismissively, turning and walking away.

"No, please, help us!" Veloria cried. Her eyes reddened and tears welled. She held out the tail feather, her eyes imploring. The short man paused and looked over his shoulder.

To Melachor and Veloria's surprise, the feather began changing colour. Within moments, it had turned from white to green.

9

The Imp looked at the feather and then at Veloria. "Quickly! Put that away!"

Veloria recoiled and tucked the feather back into her shawl, glancing over her shoulder. The Imp flicked his head to beckon them and led them down the alley he had come from.

They followed him silently as he made several turns before stopping at a nondescript door.

After glancing up and down the alley, he pushed it open and led them all in. A single candle cast eerie shadows in the dimly lit room, and a musty odour hung in the air.

A bolt of lightning lit up the alley. It was soon followed by thunder and rain as the little man pushed the door closed and whispered. "We must be quick. He has eyes everywhere. We can't be too careful. Here, show me the child. Quickly!"

Melachor and Veloria looked at each other with puzzled expressions, but Veloria did as she was asked and laid Sandor on a table. The small man looked the sickly infant up and down and smiled.

The desperate parents watched as this stranger held his hand over their baby and slowly moved it side to side. As he did, a green glow engulfed him. The mysterious light seemed to be coming from Sandor himself.

Within seconds, the child fell quiet and stopped whimpering. His breathing improved. Melachor looked on with wide eyes and open mouth. The man stopped moving his hand from side to side and held it directly above Sandor. The green glow subsided before disappearing altogether.

"You're a Metamorph?" Melachor said, looking at the Imp.

The man raised his finger to his lips and lowered his brow. He took a step back from the table and, to their amazement, began growing taller. His face stretched and his hair grew longer and changed colour. Jared, still clutching at his mother's hand, shuffled behind her.

After a few seconds, the transformation was complete. In place of an Imp, a fully grown Woodsman now looked down at the toddler and smiled.

"Don't be afraid, my young friend. You're all safe here," he said softly. He turned to Melachor and said, "But you must go, now. It's not safe for me to remain here for too long. I must leave you."

"Our son?" Melachor asked quickly, motioning to the cooing child on the table.

"The child is well now. Please, I must go before I am found. If He learns one of my kind is here, it will not be safe for any of the Imps that live here and I cannot put them in harm's way."

The man took another step back and began shrinking again. He carried on shrinking, and within seconds he morphed into a Chirvel. The furry forest animal stood on its hind legs, no taller than a chair. It squealed and sniffed the air before scurrying off into the dark.

Melachor and Veloria took Sandor and Jared and left. Melachor held his cloak over his family to shield them from the downpour. They went down the alley and tried to find their way out of the maze of backstreets. Melachor led his family through the ghetto and into the main square.

Before them was a scene of total devastation. Bodies littered the ground everywhere.

An Imp came running towards them screaming. "Quickly. Hide! He'll kill you. He'll kill us all!"

Melachor grabbed the man by the shoulders and tried to speak sense to him but he tore himself free and ran off screaming again.

Suddenly, a blinding ball of light came flying through the air and struck the fleeing Imp in the back. As it hit him, he and the ball of light both disappeared into thin air. Melachor squinted in disbelief. Several more Imps emerged from various alleyways. They, too, were screaming in panic. More blinding balls of light emerged and struck them each in quick succession. Just as before, they vanished as each ball of light struck.

Melachor hurried his family out of the square and towards the edge of the town. Every few seconds, they heard the sound of screaming followed by silence. Each time this happened, a streak of light illuminated the stormy sky. One by one, all the Imps of the Southern Tip were being wiped out.

The family rounded a corner and found their path blocked by a Trader huddled in a dark cloak. He was kneeling on the ground, holding a crystal orb in one hand. The man was muttering an incantation. As he did so, the orb began pulsating with flashes of light and a swirling vortex formed above it. Through the vortex, Melachor could see a field of green bathed in sunlight. The man stood up, glanced over his shoulder and jumped into the vortex.

Melachor turned to Veloria. Over her shoulder, he could see a blinding ball of light coming towards them. Veloria turned and screamed. Before any of them could react, the ball of light struck her. She and the two children vanished.

"NOOOO!" Melachor yelled. Tears streamed down his face and he stood there with his arm held out to where his wife and children had been standing.

Then another ball of light came flying around the corner. It hovered for a second before rushing towards Melachor at high speed. He turned and looked at the vortex over the orb, which was now dissipating. Without thinking, he lunged to grab the orb just moments before the ball of light was upon him. There was a flash, and everything went black.

Christopher D. Morgan

CHAPTER ONE

The Dream

Ten years later.

Despite the legendary tales of his father's heroic death in the war against an invading tribe, Joshua clung to the hope of one day finding him alive and well. The enemy tribe was located in the far north of Forestium, many weeks' journey from Morelle, and too far for a young Woodsman to travel. Even a Raetheon, with its majestic white wings, would take many days to reach that far.

For all Joshua knew, his father could be living out his days there, possibly held captive. Perhaps he just couldn't find his way home again.

Joshua often gazed pensively into the forest canopy at the swarms of twinkling Finkle flies in the evening twilight, lost in contemplation. All he really knew was that his father never returned.

The teenager neared his seventeenth name day: the age of decision and the age at which he could attempt the ritual trials and finally be able to call himself a true Woodsman.

Joshua's thoughts dwelled more and more on his father and how proud his dad would have been to see his son complete the trials at such a young age. These thoughts disturbed the young man, and he found it increasingly difficult to sleep at night.

And his dreams were getting worse. A wave of dread washed over him at the end of each day when the evening mist settled in. It had reached the point that he no longer wanted to sleep for fear of what the next dream would bring him.

Joshua had spent the day making arrows and strings for his bow. These were some of the skills he would need to demonstrate for the upcoming trials. After a full day of practicing, he lay on his side and gazed out his open window into the distance, fighting not to sleep.

He distracted himself by trying to make out, through the thickening evening mist, which points of light were candles from other village huts and which were Finkle flies. But the soothing humming sound of the slow-flying Dengle bugs grew louder, and Joshua found he could no longer force himself to remain awake. His eyes grew heavy and he felt himself slipping away.

His dream gripped him intensely and carried him further with each passing breath. He was powerless to resist the disturbing imagery flooding his mind.

Hazy and disconnected thoughts tormented him and he tossed and turned. His head moved rapidly from side to side as his mind desperately tried to wrench him from the terrifying experience. This nightmare was far worse than anything he had previously experienced.

A dark figure swirled in front of him. It wasn't clear who or what it was, but it screamed in fits of pain and misery. The relentless sobbing and sheer agony of the poor soul tormented Joshua, but he couldn't muster the strength to intervene, paralysed by the intensity of his emotions.

Desperate to help, he wanted to reach out and comfort whoever it was. The figure came into sharp focus only briefly before fading into blurriness again.

The face was somehow familiar but only as a distant memory. Despite being fast asleep, Joshua had the sense that perhaps the figure was his father.

The man cried out Joshua's name. He seemed to be pleading for help but Joshua was still void of strength to do anything.

The swirling persisted, and as the young Woodsman's despair intensified at his failure to stop this suffering, the hazy image changed. The veil of darkness lifted and the image of the tormented figure receded, eventually fading altogether.

Joshua felt a wave of relief that he was no longer subjected to this torment. As the fog of confusion faded, he found himself sitting up in his bed with the dawn mist lifting. He looked around, sweat dripping down his cheeks, his breathing laboured.

He heard a rustle coming from somewhere but his senses had not yet fully returned. Suddenly, there was a crash, and a figure came flying through the window.

"Hey, Joshua!" Andrew blurted as he finished his favourite window-entry manoeuvre and landed on the end of the bed. "You look terrible. Are you all right?"

"What are you doing?" Joshua mumbled.

"What do you mean, what am I doing?"

"Shhhh!" Joshua said, holding his finger to his mouth. "Do you want to wake the whole house?"

"Don't tell me you've forgotten?" Andrew lowered his head and looked at his friend with raised eyebrows. "Target practice?" He went on. "Today? Remember? Come on, we don't have that much time left before the trials."

Both boys had been working hard to hone their forest talents. They had been practicing different skills each day for the past several weeks ahead of the coming trials.

"Oh, yes, that's right, target practice. Lake Morelle." Joshua snapped out of his nightmare and was mostly himself again.

"Well?" Andrew demanded eagerly. "What are you waiting for, an invitation? Let's get going!"

Joshua grabbed his keeper bag and weapon belt. The two of them crept through the window and out onto the roof.

CHAPTER TWO
Target practice

The two strode north into the forest and Joshua tried his best to put the nightmare out of his mind. He found the rustling of the trees comforting as the pair followed the well-trodden path, winding through the forest.

Joshua was at home here in the woodlands of Morelle and felt at one with these familiar surroundings. The morning sun pierced through the treetops and glistened on the green leaves of the hanging vines dangling from the branches.

Joshua held out his hand to the side as he walked. He liked the feel of morning dew on the leaves as he brushed past them. The forest was alive with a cacophony of noises. Two Chirvels squealed as they chased each other, leaping between branches.

The two teenagers were about an hour into their walk before the trees began thinning out and the trail became brighter. By mid-morning they had reached their intended destination: Lake Morelle.

Situated in a large clearing in the forest, the lake was a favoured hunting ground for the town's young Woodsmen. The lake encircled a small island, stretching around it like a moat, with a single Yucust tree in its centre that reached high into the sky. Thick branches spread out on either side of the tree at regular intervals. The brightly coloured Finkle nests that hung beneath the branches on vines made for excellent target practice.

The two friends scavenged for raw materials from which to make the ammunition they would use for today's target practice. The thickets of Bramock that encircle the lake were a good source of materials and various types of projectiles. A good Bramock bush would fill their quivers with a fresh source of arrows and the bark from the straight twigs was stretchy enough to weave into slingshot elastic. Bramok berries were also just about the right size and weight to use in a slingshot.

"Right, let's see if you can hit the red one on the first branch on the left." Andrew suggested.

With a mocking smile, Joshua took his slingshot from his belt and placed a ripe Bramock berry into the pouch. He took aim and launched the hard berry high into the air, across the lake towards the Yucust.

The two boys followed the trajectory of the berry all the way to the tree. It missed the target by a generous margin and landed with a splash.

"You'll never make Woodsman with an aim like that," Andrew laughed. "Are you sure you don't want to be a Tender instead? Or maybe even a Fixer?"

"There's nothing wrong with being a Fixer." Joshua snapped. "Have you ever thought where we'd be without Fixers?"

"I'm only kidding," Andrew looked around for some more Bramock berries. He found a few deep inside the same thicket he had just been plucking arrows from and loaded his slingshot. Taking aim at the same Finkle nest, he pulled the slingshot pouch back towards his cheek. Just as he was about to release it, he noticed a Raetheon perched on one of the branches higher up.

"Hey, a Raetheon!" he shouted, and readjusted his aim. "I bet you I can…"

"NO!" Joshua yelled grabbing at Andrew's extended arm just as he launched the berry. It changed his aim, and the berry flew into the lake with a splash. The Raetheon, jolted by this noise, extended its wings and leaned forward off the branch. With a shriek, it fell into a graceful glide and circled the lake.

"Why were you aiming at the Raetheon? It never did anything to hurt you!"

"What difference does it make? I didn't see you complaining about shooting the Finkles."

"That's not the same thing! Raetheons are majestic animals with real feelings. Why would you want to hurt one of them?" Joshua stared at the graceful bird, still circling in the distance under the violet sky.

"What's up with you?" Andrew asked. "You've been on edge for days now. You looked awful this morning when you woke up. You're not still having those dreams, are you?"

Joshua sighed and sat on the ground with his legs crossed. He looked down in deep thought. Andrew said nothing. Joshua knew his best friend was a good listener and would not pressure him into speaking until he was ready.

It was quiet in the clearing. The only noise was the continued shrieking of the Raetheon fading into the distance. After a few moments Joshua took a deep breath.

"I had another dream last night, about my father," he said softly. "It was a much more powerful dream this time, unlike the others."

Andrew's shoulders sank, and he sighed. The age of decision that a teenager like Joshua was nearing was normally a time in a young man's life when he got much closer to his father. The trials they were preparing for were a way to strengthen the bond between father and son.

"You've been thinking about your dad a lot, lately."

Joshua didn't reply right away. When he did, he spoke quietly.

"He'd be helping us both prepare for the trials if he were still here. You never knew your father. It's different for you. You don't have memories keeping you up at nights."

"What happened?"

Joshua stared at the ground for a moment. "Someone was in great pain." He looked Andrew in the eye and said, "I think it was my dad."

"But that's not possible. I mean, your dad died when you were very young, didn't he?"

Joshua looked up and locked his gaze on Andrew.

"I know you're trying to help, but how do I know my dad really died? I mean, all we know is that he never came back."

Joshua looked back down at the ground and started to peel the shell from the Bramock berry he was toying with.

"But what if he never actually died?" he asked, after a pause. "I mean, what if he's still, you know…"

He looked up and threw the peeled berry into the water and stared vacantly at the ripples making their way around the lake.

"How is that possible?" Andrew asked. "Surely he would have come home after all these years if he was still alive."

Joshua paused as he pondered the various options he thought might explain his father's continued absence. "He could have been held captive? Or maybe he hasn't been able to find his way home?"

Not even Joshua himself was convinced at these possibilities but he was sure there had to be an explanation other than that his father was dead. In many ways, it would have been much easier if he knew for certain his father had died, but the lack of certainty gnawed away at Joshua.

"Why did he go that far away to begin with?" Andrew asked.

"I don't know. Mum doesn't like to talk about it. Maybe I'll ask. If I ever find him."

Joshua was sure it was his father's suffering he had seen. The thought he might still be alive and, worse still, in great pain, continued to weigh heavily.

Joshua had always just accepted that his father had died, but these dreams gave him an ounce of hope to cling to that he might one day see him again.

"I have to know," Joshua said after another long pause. "I have to find out."

"What are you going to do? If you're going to do the trials this year, there's only a few weeks left."

Joshua didn't respond right away. He didn't know what he was going to do, but he knew it had to be something. After pondering the question for a few more moments, he stood up with a sense of purpose.

"I'm going to find him. If there's a chance he's alive, then I have to find him. I can always do the trials next year. It'll give me a chance to improve my aim anyway."

"But you don't even know where to start looking." Andrew said, rising to his feet.

Joshua gave Andrew a resigned look. He knew his best friend was right. He didn't have any idea where to begin his search. Forestium was a big place and not without its dangers.

"I know, I'll talk to the Elder." Joshua stated with wide eyes. "Maybe he will tell me more about what happened, and when and why my dad went off to fight. It's as good a place as any to start."

With a renewed sense of purpose, the boys set off back towards Morelle.

CHAPTER THREE
Galleon

Joshua was brimming with enthusiasm as he and Andrew walked back towards the village.

"I've never seen you so excited." Andrew said as the two of them chatted about how Joshua might go about finding his father.

"I wonder what my dad looks like, now. I mean, do you think he's changed a lot over the years?"

"You really are convinced you'll find him still alive, then?"

"Why else would I see him in my dream? I bet it'll make mum so proud to see us walking back to the village together."

"Do you think he'll recognise you?"

Joshua stopped and stared into nothingness for a few moments. He looked at Andrew and shrugged. The two boys debated the issue as they walked along the winding trail.

They were about an hour outside of Morelle when they heard a rustle. They both froze. They looked at each other with lowered brows. There was the noise again, like someone or something was struggling. It was coming from just ahead of them but they couldn't see much through the mist.

As they continued, they saw what looked like an animal caught in a trapper's net strung beneath the branch of a tree.

"Is that a Wood-boar?" Andrew whispered.

"Doesn't look like Wood-boar to me."

"You're right. That's definitely not a Wood-boar. It looks more like…like…a man?"

"If it is, it's the tiniest man I've ever seen."

The small man lashed out, trying to escape from the all-encompassing net.

They crept forward.

"Hello?" Joshua called out, maintaining a safe distance.

Whoever it was stopped flailing about and froze. The man's head turned and peered at Joshua. He had deep green eyes and a small round face with large pointed ears sticking out from either side of his head.

"Well?" he called out with a ringing tone of indignation. "Are you two blithering idiots just going to stand there? You are Woodsmen, right? Surely at least one of you has something in your keeper bag to get me out of this infernal contraption?"

Joshua turned to his friend and saw a distrustful look in his eyes.

"What are you doing stuck in that Wood-boar trap?" Andrew yelled. "Wood-boars might be difficult to catch, but only an idiot would get caught in a trap like this."

There was a brief pause before the man spoke again.

"Oh, well, it's just that it's terribly comfortable here, and I thought I'd just hang around for a rest," he said rolling his eyes. "You see, it's been a long day, and I was tired and needed a place to relax. Get me out of the damned thing!"

Joshua and Andrew looked at each other again and rolled their eyes. Joshua reached for his slingshot and loaded one of the Bramock-bush arrows into in. He aimed the arrow at the vine from which the net was dangling and released it. With a swish, it sliced through the vine and the net fell to the forest floor with a thud.

"Ouch!"

Joshua and Andrew scrambled to help the small man from the entangling net. When he stood free he was little more than half their size.

He had a stocky build and a full head of untidy black hair. His light brown waistcoat was frayed at the edges and his long black leather boots reached up to his knees. He waddled around and brushed all the leaves from his clothing.

"What are you?" Andrew asked, looking the strange creature up and down.

"Isn't it usually polite to ask someone's name before you ask what kind of creature they are? Honestly! Don't they teach manners anymore?"

"Don't mind him," Joshua spoke up. "It's just that we've never met anyone of your kind before."

"Ah," the man said with a heavy sigh, looking at the ground. "I was hoping you weren't going to say that."

He walked over to a nearby tree stump, sat down and removed one of his boots. Tipping it upside down, he emptied several small pebbles out of it.

"I had hoped there would be others of my kind around these parts." He rubbed his sore foot.

"And just exactly what is your kind?" Andrew asked, walking around the short man and studying him closely.

"I'm an Imp," he replied. "You can call me Galleon." He stared at Joshua. "Galleon the Great."

Andrew let out an involuntary snigger. Joshua nudged him in the ribs. He then walked over and extended a hand to Galleon.

"I'm Joshua. This is Andrew, my best friend. Did you say you were an Imp?"

Galleon looked Joshua up and down, shaking his hand.

"That's right, and you say you've never seen anyone like me before? Well, that's a disappointment, but I can't say I'm surprised. It's been the same story everywhere I've been for years now." Galleon sighed in a resigned tone.

"I've been searching for others of my kind for a long time and to be honest, I'm starting to lose hope."

Joshua took his water sack from his belt and handed it to the stranger. Galleon regarded it before thanking him and taking several large gulps from it.

"That's better. Thank you," he said handing it back and wiping his face with the sleeve of his tunic. "It's not often I find anyone willing to be helpful or friendly towards me."

"Why not?" Joshua exclaimed with a puzzled expression.

"Well, Joshua," Galleon sighed, "that's a very good question. If ever I have a good answer, I'll let you know. As if it wasn't bad enough that all the other Imps have been banished or killed or worse, I often have to put up with mistrust and loathing wherever I go. I mean really! Is my face that bad?"

"What happened to your people?"

"The Goat killed off all my people. I'm starting to think I'm the only one of my kind left."

"Um…the Goat?" Andrew asked with raised brow.

"You've never heard of the Goat, my friend? Well, consider yourself lucky. You can think yourselves very fortunate indeed if you can live out your days without encountering the Goat."

Joshua didn't know who or what this Goat was, but judging by Galleon's face and tone, the Imp had a deep loathing for Him.

"The Goat is the most malicious, evil and angry creature you could ever wish to meet," Galleon complained. He shook his head and stared into nothingness.

"He's an all-powerful magical creature who will torture and torment you for the sheer pleasure of it." Galleon frowned and his bottom lip quivered. He went on to explain in great detail how his kind had lived in peace for many years in the grasslands of the South before they encountered the Goat.

"A Trader came through one day and brought with him some sort of mystical orb," Galleon explained. "It was supposed to be one of several that exist throughout Forestium."

"I've never heard of any mystical orb things," Andrew said narrowing his eyes.

"Yes, well, I imagine I could fill several books with all the things a worldly Woodsman of your years has never heard of."

"Go on," Joshua said, ignoring the indignant look on Andrew's face.

"Anyway, the orbs existed as mere legend until this one showed up, so you can imagine just how much of a stir it caused. Well, this Trader swore the orb had magical powers and that it could transport you to distant lands. He offered to trade it with the Imps."

"So you traded for the orb?" Andrew asked.

"Well, not exactly. As it turned out, the poor man had an unhealthy appetite for the finer things in life, especially wine, which he drank like there was no tomorrow. He was found slumped over the table one morning at an inn. Some say he died from drinking too much wine, but if you believe that, I have a Raetheon that lays golden eggs you can buy."

"You mean, he was killed?" Andrew said with his jaw open and wide eyes. Galleon nodded.

"Anyway, when they looked into the orb, what they saw was not a distant land. It was the hideous image of the Goat peering back at them. He was an evil-looking half man, half creature with long, curved horns coming out the sides of his head. Anyway, one by one, all the Imps disappeared and before too long they had all vanished. Imps are gentle and kind creatures. We didn't possess the power or magic to withstand the onslaught of the Goat."

"I've never heard of this Goat. Have you?" Joshua said, glancing at Andrew, who shook his head.

"Well anyway," Galleon continued, "it wasn't known whether the Imps were all killed or just banished to a different realm. It happened so fast. Before anyone realised what was going on, the Imps had all but been wiped out."

Galleon shook his head and heaved a sigh. "Maybe some managed to find refuge in far-flung corners of Forestium. If any did, I haven't found them yet and I've been travelling around for so long, I've seen Ashfer trees shoot up, grow old and die."

"How long has it been since you last saw another Imp?" Joshua asked with wide eyes and his mouth open.

Galleon looked pensive for a moment before speaking. "Oh, getting on for ten years I think."

"That's awful."

"It's tragic." Galleon finished putting his boot back on and stood up. "What's awful is having been strung up in that infernal Wood-boar trap for the past six hours. If it weren't for you boys strolling by, I'd still be hanging there."

"Six hours? You must be starving. You should come with us back to the village. I'm sure the Tenders there will take good care of you."

"Well, you did rescue me," Galleon admitted. "And it's been so long since anyone offered me hospitality. I'd hate to pass up the opportunity." And with that, the three of them continued on towards Morelle.

Christopher D. Morgan

CHAPTER FOUR
The Elder

When Joshua, Andrew and Galleon arrived in Morelle it was already past mid-day, and the village bustled with activity. Streams of sunlight pierced the treetop canopy high above to reveal several dozen huts and other small buildings. Kids were running about playing, and Traders pushed their carts along the main track through the centre of the village. A dozen or more Traders and Woodsmen were sitting at tables outside Morelle's only inn. They were chatting and laughing with each other.

It wasn't long before the new stranger attracted attention. Galleon looked at the people staring at him. He shuffled behind Andrew.

"Um…are you sure this is okay?"

Andrew put his arm on Galleon's shoulder and smiled at him.

"Come on, let's see if we can find you something to eat."

He walked Galleon over to one of the larger wooden huts and introduced their new friend to some of the village Tenders who, just as Joshua had predicted, immediately took to him and fed him a hearty meal. Just for good measure, they gave his clothes and hair a thorough cleaning, too.

Joshua, in the meantime, needed to see his mother. He had spoken to her before of wanting to head out into Forestium once he completed the trials, so he knew it wouldn't come as a complete surprise. He knew this would still be difficult, though.

He didn't tell his mother of his dream. He was unsure how she would react if she heard about his nightmares and his belief his father could be alive. She had already grieved for her husband and had finally come to terms with her loss. There was a loneliness in her eyes, and Joshua didn't want to cause her unnecessary heartache by mentioning his father.

When he broke the news to her, Joshua's mother kept her gaze on her son. "When will you leave?" She clutched to her chest a toy doll he used to play with, and he saw how saddened she was by this news.

"Right away. I'm leaving today. But I must first speak to the village Elder. I…I need some guidance."

"Of course. How long will you be gone? Where will you go?"

Joshua realised he had no answers prepared for all her questions.

"I…I'm not sure yet," he stammered, trying to avoid eye contact. Not only was he unsure where he was going or how long he would be away, he was also trying not to let on the true nature of his quest.

"It won't be too long," he said, trying to convince his mother, if not himself, that this was all perfectly normal. It was all he could do to hold back his own welling tears. The last thing he wanted was to upset his mother.

"I'll be back before you know it," he said, attempting an upbeat tone. "I'll speak to the Elder and then, well, I'll see you before I go."

Joshua continued to prepare things for his journey. It was awkward to look his mother in the eye and the tinkering around helped keep his attention on something else.

He gave his mother a hug that lingered longer than normal and left the hut. Joshua had fond memories of his childhood home. He would miss the safety and security it provided but he was maturing, and it was time for him to face more important issues in his life.

The thought of how happy his mother would be at the sight of him returning to Morelle, arm in arm with his father, gave him the courage he needed to embark on his journey.

He made his way through the village towards the central crossroads, where the main cluster of buildings could be found. Wooden trading carts pulled by powerful forest Shires were crisscrossing as they moved up and down the two main roads that met at the intersection.

It was a crisp day with sunlight shining all the way down to the forest floor. The ever-present light haze was drifting through the village. A group of Traders and a handful of Woodsmen were sitting at tables outside the tavern across the road. One of the Traders had brought some sort of wine back from a recent trading trip and was showing it to the others. Judging by the commotion, it seemed to be going down well.

Children were running about playing. One of them had strung a vine over a low-hanging tree branch and they were all taking turns pushing each other on this makeshift swing.

One of the more prominent buildings was a large hut made from logs and other forest materials, similar to the other Morelle dwellings. It was held together with vines and had a roof covered in moss. It appeared to have grown right out of the ground. A lantern hung on either side of the door. Joshua could smell the wax from the thick candles that were usually kept burning throughout the night. He was pleased to see white smoke billowing from the chimney, which showed that the village Elder was present.

He walked up to the front door but stopped just short of entering. It was scary. What if the Elder was in a bad mood or had no time for him?

He wanted to knock and go in but hesitated. It occurred to him that he was unprepared for what he might say to the Elder.

Joshua's enthusiasm had sustained him up until this point, but this was the moment where it might all come unravelled. Thoughts of his father and his dream rushed through his mind, and he took a deep breath. He raised his hand to the door and hesitated.

Someone inside called out, "Come, Joshua," in a reassuring voice. He recognised it. He heaved a sigh of relief and a smile spread across his face. It was the Elder, and he was not in a bad mood. Joshua pushed the door open and walked through.

Inside was dark and Joshua could smell smoke. He looked around but his eyes were still adjusting to the darkness and he couldn't see anyone so he went in farther, pulling the door closed behind him.

There were no rooms or windows, just an open space with a table and a few chairs to fill the spartan hut. What light there was came from a fireplace on the far side of the room.

The Elder's dwelling was filled with the sound of crackling from the fire's burning embers. Its dancing flames cast eerie shadows on the walls and up into the vaulted ceiling, which was held in place with large wooden beams.

"Come, Joshua," the gentle voice called again. "Come and warm yourself by the fire."

Joshua crept towards the crackling flame. As he got closer, he could see the silhouette of the Elder, sitting on a cushion of hay in front of the fire.

Joshua's eyes adjusted to the light as he neared the open flame. The Elder looked very old and frail, with long grey hair hanging down to his waist. A blanket was wrapped around his shoulders and he was rocking slowly and rhythmically back and forth, staring into the open flame.

"Elder?" Joshua asked, his voice a mere whisper. It was an honour to be granted an audience with the Elder and this was the first time Joshua had been invited to sit with him. In fact, he wasn't even sure what the correct protocol was.

The Elder turned and looked Joshua straight in the eye. He was a very old man with skin sagging from his face and crystal clear blue eyes. He looked like a stiff breeze would knock him over but at the same time he conveyed a sense of majesty and wisdom. Joshua felt humbled.

"I've been expecting you, Joshua," the Elder said in a faint voice. He patted the cushion next to him with his palm. "Come and sit down and you can tell me all about your dream."

Joshua's eyes widened. He hadn't told anyone other than Andrew about his recurring nightmares, and there was no way Andrew would have told the Elder.

He wondered if this might just have been a coincidence and the Elder wasn't really aware of his dream at all. Perhaps the Elder had just assumed this. After all, dreams happen all the time.

The Elder looked towards the fire again and continued to sit there rocking back and forth. After a couple of minutes, Joshua wondered whether he should say something, but the orange flames were captivating and the warmth felt pleasant on his face and arms. It was comforting, like hearing the soothing sound of a swarm of Dengles at night sending him off to sleep.

After a while, the Elder broke the silence. "I remember your father well," he said with a gentle nod, all the while staring into the flame. "He was a great Woodsman and brave Warrior."

Joshua's jaw dropped and he leaned closer. He had not spoken to anyone other than Andrew about his dream and had never mentioned his father to the Elder before, so it was all the more curious the Elder chose this subject to start the conversation.

"Elder, I think my father may still be alive. I think he may be in great suffering, and I need your help to find him."

The Elder said nothing, but continued instead to rock rhythmically, staring into the flame. Joshua sat and waited for a response but there was none and he was starting to get frustrated.

"I'm keen to start on my journey, Elder. Can you help me?"

After a long time the Elder spoke, "I cannot help you find what you seek."

Joshua's heart sank. He lowered his head and sighed. He worried his journey would be over before it had even begun.

After a few moments, Joshua started to rise but just as he put his palm down to the floor, the Elder spoke again.

"There will be many dangers for you ahead, Joshua, but if the answer to your dream is what you desire, you must head east to the Valley of Moross. There you must find the Oracle of Forestium."

Joshua perked up and his heart raced. He had not heard of the Oracle or of the Valley of Moross, but it didn't matter. This gave him something to go on. It was a direction to start in and a goal to reach.

Joshua was filled with a burst of energy, and he waited with bated breath to hear what else the Elder might have to say.

"The Oracle will guide you on your path," the Elder went on. "But beware; the knowledge she can give you will come at a great price."

Joshua stared at the old man with his mouth open, hanging on the wise man's every word. After a few more minutes, the Elder's eyelids lowered and his head fell forward. He appeared to slip into a deep sleep.

Joshua's thoughts raced. The Elder had given him all the information he was going to. He quietly pushed himself up and tiptoed back towards the door.

As he walked outside and closed the door behind him, he could see Andrew and Galleon sitting at one of the tables outside the tavern across the road. He walked over and joined them.

Christopher D. Morgan

CHAPTER FIVE
Leaving Morelle

"I've just been talking to the Elder," Joshua blurted out. "He said I had to seek the Oracle in some place called the Valley of Moross. I don't even know where that is."

"I do," Galleon said. "It's a long way from here, over to the east."

"Can you take me there?"

Galleon considered the idea for a few moments before shaking his head.

"You? Not likely." He turned back and took a swig from his ale. "It's too far, and a child like you is not up to the journey." He gulped down the last drop from the mug. "There are more dangers in Forestium than a young Woodsman like you could shake a stick at. You'd be chewed up and spat out before you know it."

Joshua was still brimming with excitement, and his enthusiasm wasn't going to be dampened.

"Have you ever been there?" Joshua asked.

"Well, no."

"Didn't you say you were looking for others of your kind?"

"Yes," Galleon squinted. "Why do you ask?"

"Well, there may be others of your kind living in the Valley of Moross."

Andrew looked at Galleon with a wry smile. "He has you there."

"It stands to reason you'll need to visit there sooner or later." Joshua continued. "You said yourself it's dangerous, so why don't we go there together and look out for each other? Perhaps the Oracle can help us both."

Galleon said nothing but continued to stare at Joshua. He pursed his lips and took a deep breath. "Hmmm. You might be young and ill prepared," the Imp finally said, "but you do make a valid point. I should warn you I've never been a good babysitter, so you'll have to pull your own weight when we're on the road."

Galleon took another deep breath, exhaled, and slammed his mug down onto the table. "OK, then. Let's go and find this Oracle."

Galleon and Joshua shook hands and Joshua beamed. They both got up and Galleon went inside the tavern, leaving Joshua and Andrew together.

Joshua turned to Andrew. Andrew looked at Joshua and his smile faded.

"What's the matter?" Joshua asked.

"What do you mean, what's the matter?" Andrew snapped. "You're going away, that's what's the matter. I haven't even had any time to get used to the idea. And what if you don't come back?"

Joshua thought about this. It was all happening very fast, and he hadn't had time to think about the consequences of his quest or the dangers he would face along the way.

He and Andrew had grown up together and they were much more than just best friends. The thought of having to say goodbye to everyone, especially to Andrew, started hitting home too.

"I have to do this, Andrew. I have to find my dad. If he really is suffering, I couldn't live with myself if I didn't do anything about it."

"You could be gone for ages!" Andrew shouted. He turned and ran off down the path, disappearing into the mist.

Joshua wanted to run after him but felt it would only make him feel worse. It was also a very painful realisation for Joshua that he might, indeed, not see his best friend for some time.

Galleon came out of the tavern and said, "Right, when do we leave? Hey, why the long face? You look like a Wood-boar that's just realised he's the main course at dinner."

Joshua paused for a few seconds, still gazing at where Andrew had disappeared into the mist, and said, "Right away. I just need to say goodbye to my mother. Then we can go."

The two made their way over to the village hall, where his mother and many of the other Tenders of Morelle were waiting to say their farewells to Joshua. As they approached the centre of town, there was already a crowd of people assembling. Joshua stopped briefly and Galleon looked at him.

"Are you OK?" Galleon asked.

Joshua smiled and said, "I've watched this going-away ritual many times before, but never thought it might one day be me saying goodbye. It just feels strange, that's all."

Everyone gave Joshua hugs and wished him the best. Each time he embraced another village Tender, he looked around to see if he could see Andrew, but his best friend was nowhere to be found. It looked like his last memory of Andrew for the foreseeable future would be of his friend storming off, upset.

The last person Joshua said goodbye to was his mother. Full of emotion, she flung her arms around him. She squeezed him so tight he could hardly breathe, but it felt good all the same.

Barely audible, Joshua's mother whispered into his ear, "Please come back safely, Joshua, I cannot bear the thought of losing you too."

Joshua looked at his mother and saw the heartache in her eyes. He expected her to be upset at his leaving, but there was something else: something he couldn't quite put his finger on.

Not wanting to prolong the farewell, he gave his mother one last kiss and a hug. With a final wave, he and Galleon headed off down the path and out of the village of Morelle, not knowing when, or indeed if, he would return.

As the familiar sounds of the village faded behind them, Joshua looked back several times hoping to see Andrew, but was disappointed each time.

The two new travelling companions walked in silence for the first couple of hours until they reached the outer boundary of Morelle. Joshua was sad at having to leave his village, his mother and Andrew, but didn't want to let on to Galleon. He wanted to show him he was strong and ready for whatever lay ahead.

Every so often, Galleon would glance at Joshua and then look ahead again. Joshua knew Galleon wanted to say something, but was glad he didn't. This was a painful process for Joshua, and he was glad Galleon was not pressing the issue.

It was another hour before Joshua started a conversation. "So, how are we going to get to the Valley of Moross?"

Galleon pondered this for a moment. "We head east. The Valley of Moross sits between two mountain ranges."

"How far is it?"

"Well, I've never actually been there so I'm not sure. I guess we'll find out when we get there, if we don't fall off the edge of the world first, that is."

Suddenly, they heard a faint voice in the distance behind them.

"Stop!"

Joshua and Galleon halted and looked at each other.

"Did you hear that?" Joshua asked, turning to look in the direction the sound came from. The voice sounded again, but this time it was louder.

"Stop! Wait for me!"

Joshua peered into the distance. A figure emerged through the thick mist. He'd recognise that brown hair and stocky frame anywhere. A smile formed across his face. It was Andrew running towards them. Puffing and panting, he caught up with them.

"What are you doing here?" Joshua asked.

"You didn't think I'd let you have all the fun, did you?" Andrew said, still panting. "Besides, with your aim, there's no way you'd survive without me. I'm coming with you."

"You don't have to do this, Andrew. This isn't your journey. I don't want you to get hurt."

"Look," Andrew said, cutting him off. "We've been best friends for as long as I can remember. I can't think of anywhere I'd rather be than by your side."

Galleon rolled his eyes and shook his head. "Well, if the two of you are going to insist on kissing, then I may have to throw up. Shall we go?"

The two young Woodsmen looked at each other and beamed.

"Well, come on then, boys," Galleon said. "We'll never get there at this rate."

All three of them set off.

CHAPTER SIX
Sarah

Joshua and Andrew's initial excitement about the journey faded the farther they went from Morelle. The three travellers walked for several days without encountering another soul. This was much farther than Joshua or Andrew had ever ventured outside of Morelle and they found their surroundings to be unnerving.

Then the thick vegetation they were struggling through opened up and they wandered into an eerie forest clearing. They walked closer to each other. Something just didn't seem right. The trees were not the same. There was an unpleasant odour in the air and even the forest litter beneath their feet sounded different; it was somehow unsettling.

The mood changed. Something was amiss. Joshua slowed to a crawl and held his hand up, surveying the clearing.

The trio stopped walking and Galleon stopped talking. The sun shone down into the forest clearing, and there was a faint humming in the air. They could hear the distant shrieking of a Raetheon soaring somewhere high up. Raetheons usually shrieked when they were scared, and this did nothing to ease the tension. The three continued to creep into the forest clearing.

"Someone's here," Andrew whispered. He scanned the clearing. Galleon glanced at him and then looked around, his eyes darting from tree to tree.

"Are you sure?" Galleon whispered back. He narrowed his eyes and scanned the perimeter of the clearing.

They all crept on farther. Galleon stepped on a twig. It broke in two and made a loud snapping sound. There was a swishing noise and a swift rush of wind. Before any of them could react, a huge net lifted up around them and engulfed their bodies.

They dangled in the air several feet above the ground. As they struggled in vain to free themselves, a figure covered in twigs and grass rose from the ground right below them.

"Oh, hello. Sorry, I wasn't expecting people," came a soft, high-pitched voice.

Joshua, Andrew and Galleon stopped struggling and stared at this curious mass of bush and twigs.

"I was really hoping for a Wood-boar, but it seems the three of you accidentally wandered into my trap. Well, it's not a real trap. Well, I suppose it is but it's not a very good one, I guess. I mean if it were a good trap, I'd have caught a Wood-boar days ago but I haven't caught anything yet. I'm normally really good at catching things you know. Once, I caught a Raetheon accidentally. You see, it had a broken wing and, well, it sort of stumbled into the trap accidentally. I didn't mean to hurt it, of course. I wasn't really trying to catch it, you see…"

"Um, sorry, but, who are you?" Joshua interrupted.

"More to the point, can you please get us out of this infernal thing? Honestly!" Galleon said.

"Oh, um, yes, well, that's probably a good idea. What must you think of me? I mean, I suppose it must look rather rude of me to stand here talking whilst you're still hanging there. I mean, it can't be very comfortable for you in there, can it and, well…"

"Ahem!" Andrew snapped.

"Oh, yes, sorry. Here, let me cut you down."

The mass of twigs and straw pulled out a slingshot and arrow. With one swift arm action, it launched the arrow and sliced straight through the vine from which the net was suspended. The whole contraption fell to the ground with a thud.

"Ouch! Couldn't you have landed on him instead?" Galleon shouted.

The three captives flailed around untangling the net and picking themselves up off the ground. They looked at the mass of twigs and straw, still somewhat dazed from the experience.

"Sorry," Joshua said, "but who or what are you?"

"Hmm? Oh, sorry," the mass of twigs replied with a giggle. And with that, a pair of hands emerged and pulled away the makeshift camouflage suit revealing a young woman. As she removed the headpiece of spiky grass she shook her head to reveal beautiful blond hair that fell to her shoulders and down her back. She looked at Joshua and smiled.

"I'm Sarah," she said extending her hands out to either side.

Joshua stood there captivated. She had deep blue eyes and a small, round face with rosy cheeks and a petite pointed nose. A straight fringe of fine hair hung just above her eyes. Joshua thought she was the most beautiful thing he had ever seen. For a moment, he lost track of time, where he was or even that he had moments before been held upside down in her trap. He wanted to speak. He opened his mouth but was unable to produce any words.

Sarah giggled. The infectious sound made his heart race.

"What are you doing here?" Andrew demanded.

"Oh, well, I'm out on an expedition to learn new skills. I'm a Fixer. Well, I'm learning to be a Fixer that is. I mean I am really a Fixer but I've just not done the trials yet. I've been gone for several months already and, well, at least I think it's been several months. It's so difficult to keep track of time, you see. I did have a piece of string I was using to track the number of days and, well, I sort of lost it wrestling an injured Raetheon. It had a broken wing and fell into my trap, you see…"

"Do you mean to say you've been out here alone for months?" Andrew asked, interrupting Sarah's runaway enthusiasm. Neither he nor Joshua had ever been away from their village for more than a few days.

Sarah giggled yet again. "Yes, that's right. I did think about going back to my village a few times but, well, I'm not entirely sure where I am anymore and, well, I'm really enjoying myself anyway. You see, I'm learning new skills all the time. Take this trap, for example; I've been perfecting it over the past few days. Well, it's not perfect yet or I would have caught a Wood-boar. Still, it did catch the three of you. Did I tell you I accidentally caught a Raetheon once? It had a broken wing and, well…"

"Do you always talk this much?" Andrew sneered.

"Don't be rude, Andrew!" Joshua said, nudging him in the ribs. Although he turned his head in Andrew's direction to deliver this admonishment, he kept his eyes trained on Sarah.

"I'm Joshua, and this is Andrew."

"Hello, Joshua," Sarah replied. "And who is this little boy you have with you?" Sarah bent towards Galleon and pinched his cheek.

"I'm not a little boy!" Galleon retorted pulling his cheek free. "I'm an Imp. I don't suppose you've ever seen anyone like me before either, then?"

He didn't bother waiting for an answer and started walking around brushing debris from his hair.

"Really?" Sarah said in wonder, her eyes wide. "I've heard of Imps but I've never seen one before."

Galleon stopped brushing himself down and looked at Sarah. "You know about Imps?" he asked raising his eyebrow.

"Well, only the stories I've been told. I thought all the Imps were gone."

"Hmmm. Well, not all of them," Galleon said, continuing to pull twigs out of his hair.

"Where are you going?" Joshua asked Sarah.

Andrew's shoulders sank, and he rolled his eyes. He crossed his arms and glared at Joshua. Joshua ignored him.

"Well, nowhere in particular really. I'm travelling around all over and learning new skills. I've learnt so much already but I do really need to perfect my trap-building skills. I've been trying to trap a Wood-boar, you see and, well…"

"Why don't you come with us?"

Andrew's shoulders sank still further, and he rolled his eyes again, this time shaking his head at the same time.

"We're heading to the Valley of Moross," Joshua added, continuing to ignore Andrew. "I bet you'll learn loads of things along the way."

Joshua not only found Sarah very attractive but he was also impressed with her resourcefulness. Anyone that could survive on her own for as long as she already had was bound to make for an excellent travelling companion.

"I'm sure Galleon would also love to hear everything you know about Imps. Right Galleon?" He turned to Galleon and nodded with raised eyebrows. Galleon nodded back.

"Hmm, I've never been that far east before, and I have always wanted to see the mountains. Sure, why not?"

The four of them set off out of the clearing and into the mist. Sarah told them all about the stories she had heard about Imps from the various Traders she had encountered on her travels. Andrew just sighed and continued to shake his head.

CHAPTER SEVEN
Fable & Florelle

The four travellers continued to move east towards the Valley of Moross. Joshua listened with fascination as Sarah recounted stories about all the new skills she had acquired. By all accounts, despite her being no older than himself, Sarah was already a very accomplished Fixer.

She could not only hunt but was able to fashion weapons from just about anything at hand. She told them all about the different types of vines she had found and how she used these to make slingshots and bowstrings.

Galleon at one point snagged his tunic on a hooked Bintok vine. Within minutes, Sarah found a Sprinkle bush and stripped out one of the inner spikes to use as a needle. She removed the outer skin of a twig from one of the Sprinkle bush branches and stripped it into fine thread. She then used that to sew up Galleon's tunic until it was like new again.

Joshua looked on with raised brows. The whole thing took no more than a couple of minutes, with little fuss. Joshua and Galleon smiled at each other with jaws dropped.

Galleon and Sarah were getting along very well. She was the first person he had encountered for many years who had heard of Imps. Joshua could see him reacting to her warm and bubbly attitude.

Andrew seemed mostly irritated with Sarah's tendency to talk endlessly about everything and nothing. He didn't find anything she did impressive. Every time she demonstrated one of her amazing abilities, he rolled his eyes and pulled a scornful face. Joshua thought it was just jealousy.

After a few more days of travelling, the four adventurers stumbled upon an inn. It was a decent sized log hut, not unlike those Joshua was familiar with from Morelle.

It was surrounded by a gaggle of small forest creatures. There were several baby Raetheons wandering around picking for Dengle grubs on the ground. Some of the Raetheons had bandages on their wings and or were limping.

A hairy Wood-boar was tied to the leg of one of several tables in front of the inn. The lumbering beast was waddling about trying to catch the Raetheons as they foraged for food. It had a bandage on its hind leg and was unable to move fast enough for the more agile birds. Despite the menacing fangs, it looked fairly tame as it nosed around in the dirt for grubs.

A pair of Chirvels was sitting on their hind legs on the roof of the inn. They were peering in opposite directions as they often did, scouting for full-grown Raetheons that might swoop in and catch them. Several more Chirvels were gnawing at leftover scraps on the tables below the two lookouts.

Above the inn door hung a sign that read 'Fable & Florelle's Inn - the best Wood-wine in all of Forestium'. There was nobody else about but as they got closer, the door opened and a stout, round man came out. He was a portly figure with a gruff beard.

He wore an apron around his waist, smeared with food stains.

"Clear 'oof you little scoundrels!" he shouted in a moody voice, waving at the adorable, furry Chirvels. They scattered, barely managing to escape the back of his hand.

"Rotten vermin," he mumbled.

He cleared the table of the few mugs sitting there and wiped it down with a cloth he had strung over his shoulder. With a dissatisfied frown, he finished clearing the table and turned to go back into the inn.

With a swift sweeping motion, he launched one of the injured Raetheons out of his path with his left boot. The baby Raetheon squealed when it landed and limped off. He pushed the door open and went back inside mumbling to himself slamming the door behind him.

Joshua and Galleon looked at each other. "Charming fellow," Galleon said. "I wonder if he treats visitors like he treats forest creatures. I've eaten dried Shrooms with more charm."

"We've been walking for days," Joshua said. "We could do with a rest for a short while. Come on, let's take a look. Maybe we can get a home-cooked meal."

"It would make a change from dried Dengle grubs and Wood-shrooms," Andrew grumbled. He grimaced as if he'd just eaten something sour.

"What? Don't you like my boiled Wood-shrooms?" Sarah asked, raising her eyebrows.

Everyone was grateful for her cooking skills but they had all been hoping for a good, home-cooked meal for some time now. Joshua wondered whether Sarah picked up on Andrew and Galleon being overly polite when it came to her experimenting with new recipes.

"No, it's great." Andrew rolled his eyes at Joshua and winked. "It would just be nice to have something that didn't grow off a dead tree for a change."

Galleon nodded in agreement. "Yes, your food is…lovely," he said, doing his best to keep a straight face. "Really, who would have thought there were so many different ways of preparing boiled Wood-shrooms."

He and Andrew cast each other a glance and they both stifled a chuckle. Sarah turned to them and they both removed their smirks. She lowered her brow and pursed her lips together. Her stare lingered, and she turned her gaze back to the inn. As she did, she gave Joshua a wink, and he smiled.

Joshua walked up to the inn door and pushed it open, and they all followed him through. Inside were a number of wooden tables positioned around a central counter. Candles hung from the rafters, and more injured animals scurried about the place.

Some of the animals chirped and squealed as Galleon closed the door. A huge fireplace on the far left wall sported a raging fire, and Andrew went over to it to warm himself.

There were five or six stools around each of the ragged-looking tables. The slanted roof on both sides was quite high and there were a number of strange things hanging from the rafters. Some looked like the sort of weapons Woodsmen might use but Joshua didn't recognise many of them.

Above the counter hung a number of brown mugs as well as an assortment of other curious looking wooden objects.

The bearded man was standing behind the counter with one mug in his hand. He was wiping it with the same cloth he used to clear the table. He was peering at them with a grumpy look but didn't say anything and just carried on wiping the mug.

Judging by the man's casual attitude at seeing them walk through the door, Joshua wondered whether they would be welcome here as customers. Galleon motioned to the table closest to the fire and they each took a stool around it and sat down.

Just as they took their seats, a short and plump woman wandered into the inn from a door behind the counter. She had curls of untidy white hair and wore a pointed black hat.

"Oh, be with you in a mo, me darlings," she shouted across to them.

She took an apron from a hook on the door and wrapped it around her waist. With a broad smile, she hurried over to their table.

"Hello, me dears," she beamed with a welcoming smile. "Just look at yer rosy cheeks. You look like you could do with a nice pot of me 'ome-made stew." Her voice was soothing just like the tones of the village Tenders back home.

Galleon and Andrew beamed at each other and nodded.

"Um, that sounds lovely," Joshua said.

"FABLE!" the woman barked in needlessly demanding voice, as she turned and looked at the counter. "ONE POT OF STEW! NOW!"

Everyone at the table shrank in their seats. The man slammed the mug down and mumbled to himself as he turned and disappeared through the same door the plump woman had entered. She turned to them again and carried on, but in a motherly tone again.

"Oh dear, where's me manners?" she said in a gentle voice. "I'm Florelle, me darlings. That's Fable over there." Her tone was low and disapproving as she motioned towards the empty counter.

"I'm Joshua. This is Andrew, Sarah and Galleon." Joshua said, pointing to the others in turn.

"Oh, well, my," Florelle said with a lingering stare in Galleon's direction. "We haven't had an Imp here in these parts for many years now." She peered at him.

Galleon perked up.

"You've seen Imps before?" he asked, raising his brow and widening his eyes. "How long ago?"

"Ohhhh, not for some years now, me darling." She gazed into open space for a moment. "T'was a time when we would see Imps regularly in here but I haven't seen another for a good few years now." She looked at Galleon again. "I was beginning to wonder whether they all died out or something. Glad to see I was wrong about that." She ended with a warm smile at Galleon.

The despondent Imp's shoulders sank again, and he looked down at the table.

"How about some of our famous Wood-wine to warm yer's up?" Florelle asked with a beaming smile. Before anyone had a chance to respond, she grasped her apron, spun around towards the counter and rushed over to fetch four brown mugs.

She returned and put the mugs on the table, went back to the counter and lifted a clay pitcher from one of the hooks above it.

Hanging from a girder behind the counter was what Joshua first assumed to be a set of bellows. It looked like a big sack made of some sort of animal skin and was pointed at the bottom with a small tube extending from its lowest point.

Florelle placed the pitcher beneath it and untwisted a screw on the end of the small dangling tube. A golden liquid flowed into the pitcher. When the pitcher was full, she twisted the screw again to stop the flow of liquid and lifted the container back to their table.

"Ere...this is the reason people keep coming back ere," she beamed. "It's about the only useful thing 'ees ever done. We call it Wood-wine. It'll put 'airs on yer chests, me darlings."

She poured the golden brown liquid into each of their mugs in turn. With the pitcher still in her hands, she stood there with a brimming smile and waited for their verdict.

Galleon and Andrew looked at each other with suspicion. Galleon took his mug and sniffed its contents. The others watched with interest. He raised his eyebrows at Andrew and took a sip. It left a golden froth on his upper lip that he licked away.

"That's delicious," Galleon said to Florelle, who beamed with delight.

Andrew took a swig, and he too licked the golden froth from his lips. He then gulped the rest of it down in a single swig and once more licked the golden froth from his lips.

"Me 'usband Fable over there stumbled onto the recipe by accident," Florelle explained as she topped up Galleon and Andrew's mugs again.

"Um, why are there so many injured animals here?" Sarah asked.

At this point, Fable emerged from behind the door with a black cauldron. Steam was billowing from it and he was holding it with a thick mitten in each hand. There was so much steam rising from it that Fable found it difficult to see where he was going and stumbled several times on the way to their table.

"Well, someone's gotta look after the poor darlings, don't they? Forest creatures know to come to me and I'll fix 'em up good an' proper."

Fable snorted as he placed the large cauldron in the middle of their table. Florelle cast him a disapproving glance. Mumbling to himself, Fable sneered at his wife before walking back to the counter and rummaging beneath it.

Various things clattered to the floor before he emerged again with four bowls and spoons and brought them back to them. He tossed them onto the table in a pile before catching Florelle's eye again and walking off with another sneer.

Joshua said nothing about this lack of social graces as he passed out the bowls and spoons to the others.

Andrew and Galleon stared at the steam coming from the cauldron and licked their lips in anticipation. Florelle took the ladle and heaped generous portions into each of the bowls. Neither Andrew nor Galleon needed any further invitation; both began devouring the steaming stew.

"That's it, me darlings," Florelle said, as they lapped away. "You eat yer fill. It'll put 'airs on yer chests." She beamed another smile and went back to the counter.

They all tucked into their hot meal.

"Hmmm, this is just delicious. I've never tasted anything quite like it before," Sarah said, sipping from her spoon. "I think those are Lifren leaves," she said, leaning over her bowl and sniffing. "Those little green balls are definitely Wood-sprouts but I don't know about the stringy root things. These are Shrooms, of course, but I'm just not sure if they are from the Wendilious or Grempanian family." She took another sip from her spoon. "Hmmm, there's definitely hind leg of Wood-boar here too."

The others were much too busy eating to pay much attention, although that didn't stop her.

Both Andrew and Galleon went through no less than four full bowls before leaning back with satisfied looks on their faces.

Sarah and Joshua took much longer but still got through three bowls each. At the end of the meal, nobody was saying very much. They were all full and happy to be sitting there near the fireplace and resting.

The tranquil setting was interrupted when Florelle came in through the front door with a Raetheon chick she had picked up outside. It was shrieking and looked like it had lost half a foot.

"Oh, the poor thing," Sarah said getting up off her stool to take a look at the unfortunate, helpless creature. "What's the matter with him?"

"Fable's stinking Wood-boar out there managed to grab hold of the poor thing. I know 'ee was only being playful and all but 'ee doesn't realise 'ees own strength, you see. Not to worry, me darling," she said, looking at the distressed bird with a tender smile and soft tone, "Florelle will sort yer out."

"FABLE!" she shouted in the direction of the door behind the counter. Moments later, the Innkeeper emerged.

"Not another rotten Raetheon?" he moaned, shaking his head. "I keep telling you we'd be better off cooking and serving 'em than mending the darn things."

"Well, just maybe there might be fewer injured creatures around 'ere if you did something about that stinking Wood-boar out front."

Fable just rolled his eyes and walked out the front door, shaking his head and slamming the door shut behind him.

"What's his problem?" Andrew asked Florelle. "Is he always this grumpy?"

"I'm afraid so, me darling." She grabbed a stool and took a seat with them around the fireplace. "It's not 'ees fault. 'Ees not always been this way. Only since that rotten mirror came into our lives."

"Um, mirror?" Joshua asked, leaning forward and raising his eyebrows.

"They call it the 'Mirror of Prophecy'," Florelle replied, "It's rumoured each owner of the mirror can use it once to see into the future. A Trader arrived some years ago. In a terrible state, 'ee was. Looked to have been in a battle or something and very weak. Anyway, he stayed here for a few days but we found the poor darling dead one morning."

"Oh, that's awful," Sarah said bringing her hand to her mouth.

"Anyway," Florelle went on, nodding her head, "nobody ever came asking for this fella so we eventually went through 'ees things and found a mirror. It was wrapped in cloth. Fable unwrapped it one night and saw something unusual. 'Ee said 'ee saw 'imself die, so 'ee did. It was an 'orrible death, so 'ee said. But 'ee doesn't know how far into the future it was. So now, 'ee walks around all day in a foul mood because 'ee thinks 'ees going to die an 'orrible death but doesn't know when."

"That's…that's…well, that's terrible," Sarah said, still holding her hand to her mouth and barely able to get the words out.

"I've heard of the Mirror of Prophecy," Galleon said, breaking his silence since eating. "I didn't think it was real. Can I see it?"

"Ohhh, I don't think that's a good idea, me darling. I mean, what if it's true, and you saw something you didn't want to see?

You don't want to end up like me Fable, now do you?" Galleon pursed his lips and nodded, and didn't press the matter any further.

Florelle spent much of the evening telling the travellers about her work with injured animals and how she and Fable made a living from the Traders passing through in need of rest, a meal and a place to spend the night. Some of their regulars came from far and wide just to taste their wonderful Wood-wine.

A dozen or more Traders came and went over the course of the evening. Many of them drank copious amounts of the Wood-wine. One or two of them could barely keep upright by the time they left the inn. Some of them rented rooms for the night and one remained at his stool, lying face down on the table and clutching his last mug of the intoxicating brew. He had drunk about eight mugs as far as Joshua could tell.

Whatever it was Fable put into the wine, it took its toll on some of the Traders. They exchanged stories and showed each other the wares they had come to trade. It was mostly cloth, weapons and implements they traded with each other. The odd piece of jewellery was also brought out for inspection every now and then. Judging by the different colours of their tunics, Joshua counted Traders from eight different villages or more.

Against the back wall next to the door behind the counter was a row of small jars. As each Trader left the inn, Fable or Florelle would dip their hand into one of the jars and hand a small piece of something from the jar to the departing visitor.

"What's in the jars?" Joshua asked Florelle.

"Oh, we like to give the travellers something for their onward journey. It's liquorice moss."

"Liquorice?" Galleon said sitting upright with a burst of energy. "Did you say, liquorice?" He fixed a stare at the row of small jars.

"That's right, me darling. Would you like a piece?" Florelle asked.

Just as Galleon opened his mouth to speak, Andrew said, "I'll try a piece."

Galleon turned and looked at him as if he'd just been robbed of something valuable. Florelle walked around the counter and reached for one of the small jars and took a small piece of black liquorice moss out. She replaced the lid and brought the piece back over to their table.

Joshua was curious to see that Galleon kept his gaze transfixed on Florelle's hand as she made her way over. The Imp was holding his hands up by his chest and appeared to be standing on tiptoes. Leaning forward as Florelle handed the liquorice moss to Andrew, Galleon was practically salivating. He seemed to follow the moss with his body as he watched Andrew put the piece of stringy, black treat into his mouth.

As Andrew chewed on the moss, Galleon's mouth opened wider and his eyebrows rose in anticipation.

"That's not fair! Honestly!" the Imp suddenly blurted out. "That's mine! I want it!" he demanded. "I want it now!"

Andrew, Joshua and Sarah looked at each other with stunned expressions and then at Florelle. She smiled back at them.

"That's alright, me darlings," she said with a chuckle. "It's been years since I last saw it, but Imps can be very tempted by liquorice. Drives 'em crazy with desire, you see. Between you and me, I reckon you could get an Imp to do just about anything for the promise of a nice piece of liquorice."

All through this explanation, Galleon's eyes remained glued to Andrew chewing the liquorice moss. He seemed unaware of his surroundings. When Andrew finally swallowed the liquorice, Galleon looked sullen and deflated and his lower lip quivered.

Sarah looked at Joshua and giggled. "Best we keep that little secret to ourselves," she whispered to him. Joshua grinned and nodded.

"Tell yer what, how 'bout I get you a nice little bit of liquorice moss all for yerself, me darling," she said to Galleon, who beamed with delight and jumped up and down a couple of times clapping and nodding.

"Don't you worry, me darling, Florelle will fix yer up good 'n proper. Won't be a mo'"

Florelle went back to the counter and picked another small piece of liquorice moss from one of the jars and returned to give it to Galleon. He snatched it from her hand like a mischievous child, ran over to a quiet corner of the inn and eagerly stuffed it into his mouth.

He faced the corner and peered over his shoulder a couple of times whilst chewing on the stringy moss as if trying to guard a precious treasure. Joshua, Andrew and Sarah couldn't stop laughing.

By the end of the night, the embers in the fireplace were smouldering. The last Traders were finishing up their Wood-wine and putting on their tunics. Fable lifted the last Trader, who had been lying face down on his table, and coaxed him out the door where another Trader from his home village took over.

"You'll be wanting rooms for the night then, me darlings?" Florelle asked, as Andrew was dozing off. "I've only got two rooms left tonight so some of yer's will 'ave to be sharing."

Joshua looked at Andrew, slumped over the table. He was all but asleep already. He looked at Galleon, who shrugged his shoulders and said he was happy to sleep anywhere. He turned to Sarah. She glanced back at him, and there was an awkward moment as the two of them caught each other's eye. After a pause, they both let out a nervous giggle.

"You two will be 'aving a room together, then, me darlings?" Florelle smiled as she waved a room key towards Joshua and Sarah.

"Oh, well, um" Joshua stammered, and looking fleetingly at Sarah. "We're not, um, well…you know."

Sarah chuckled at Joshua's reddening face and ineffective attempt at clarifying the situation. Florelle just looked at him with her brow raised.

"Come on, Joshua," Galleon said after the pause was starting to get uncomfortable. "You help me get this lump of a friend of yours up and the three of us share a room. Sarah can have the other."

"Of course," Joshua said with nervous chuckle. He was glad at this distraction.

He and Sarah caught each other's eye. There was another pause in which neither of them said anything but just kept staring at each other.

"See you in the morning then, Sarah," Galleon said in a deliberate tone, once again breaking the embarrassing silence.

"Right," Sarah said, "well, good night. See you in the morning."

They made their way to their rooms and turned in for the night.

CHAPTER EIGHT

Mirror of Prophecy

Joshua woke up the following morning to find Andrew and Galleon still snoring. The thick morning mist obscured the view through the single, narrow window in their cramped room, and there was a chill in the air.

He returned to the warmth of the inn, where Fable was already putting more wood onto the fire to liven it up. The grumpy man was sitting in front of the fireplace stripping Wood-shrooms from a pile of logs stacked neatly on either side of it. A dozen or more ripe Shrooms had grown over each log. One by one he sliced the golden brown Shrooms away and dumped them into a bucket between his legs.

Once all the Shrooms were harvested, he threw each log onto the fireplace. Each one erupted into clouds of white billowing smoke for a few seconds before being engulfed by flames. After several of these logs had been stripped and thrown onto the fire Fable stood up, picked up the bucket and disappeared with it through the door behind the counter.

Joshua wondered whether the Wood-shrooms were one of the ingredients he was using to make the delicious Wood-wine. He sat there for a few moments, peering into the flames, and found his thoughts drifting to his father and the journey ahead.

It was already getting busy in the inn. A few Traders were already having breakfast eating from soup bowls. Two of them were chattering together at a table while others preferred to sit alone. A lone Trader in a far, dimly lit corner was wearing a dark cloak with a hood over his head. He stared at Joshua when he came in but then quickly looked down at his soup. Joshua squinted to get a better look at him but he was interrupted.

"Good morning," Galleon said as he wandered in stretching his arms and yawning. "Lovely beds they have here. Who knew that branches and sharp twigs could be so bleeding comfortable!" He walked over to the table where Joshua was sitting and took a seat beside him. He looked up at Joshua and winked.

For a minute, Joshua was worried Galleon was going to say something about Sarah and that awkward moment last night but he just smiled and said nothing. Joshua was relieved. Inexperienced in matters of the heart, he felt embarrassed about engaging in a conversation about his feelings for Sarah. Andrew came in wiping his eyes and took a seat by the fireplace next to them.

"Have you given any more thought to how we're going to get to the Valley of Moross?" Andrew asked.

Joshua looked into the fireplace and sighed as if hoping it would provide inspiration.

"No," he answered lowering his head. "If only we had that mirror." He looked around at the others. "If it really can show the future, we might at least know when we'll get there. How much farther is it anyway?" Joshua asked, turning to Galleon.

"Oh, still quite a few days travel yet. The River of Torrents runs north to south along the mountain pass and we'll have to cross that to get there. That's going to be about as easy as catching a wild Raetheon while blindfolded." He raised his brow and nodded.

Joshua and Andrew looked at each other and then back at Galleon.

"Just exactly why will that be so hard?" Andrew inquired, frowning.

"Because of all the Razorfins, of course. The river is full of the vicious, toothy creatures at this time of the year. A young Woodsman like yourself would make a tempting meal for a full-grown Razorfin."

Joshua and Andrew looked at each other again, wondering what a Razorfin was. Neither of them had heard of these before and had no intention of meeting one, either.

Suddenly the front door flung open, and in burst Sarah. She was cupping what looked like a wounded Raetheon in both hands. It was looking up at her and shrieking.

"Oh, hello," she said, noticing the three of them sitting by the fire. "I didn't realise you were awake. I found this little one hobbling down the path. I think he's injured. He can't be more than a few weeks old. I thought I'd bring him back here so Florelle could fix him up. Haven't seen her have you?"

The boys looked at each other and shook their heads.

"The poor thing has lost one of its toes. Not sure how it happened. I think a Wood-boar must have got it or something. Doesn't look like it's been caught in a trap. I caught an adult Raetheon in a trap once. Did I tell you? It wasn't on purpose, mind you. It sort of stumbled into it by accident. I was really trying to catch…"

"Oh, me darling, you've got another one," Florelle said to Sarah as she came through the door behind the counter and rushed over to take a look at the injured creature.

Andrew leaned towards Galleon and whispered, "Doesn't she ever shut up?"

Florelle carefully took the injured chick from Sarah and dashed behind the counter to the row of small jars on the shelf. She squinted at the jars, pointing her finger at each in turn, reading frantically from the faded labels.

"Liquorice moss, Shroom seeds, boar treats, essence of fern, ah 'ere we are, Yucust salve," she said, her finger landing on the fifth jar.

After unscrewing its lid, she reached in and wiped a dollop of the pale, gooey paste onto two fingers and then gently rubbed it onto the chick's injured foot. The frightened baby bird quivered as Florelle massaged the paste over its leg.

A few seconds later, it stretched its tiny wings and shook its head as if warding off any remaining pain. It then started cooing softly. Whatever it was in the jar, it seemed to do the trick.

"How long have you three been up?" Sarah asked as she came over to the table by the fireplace.

"Just a few minutes," Joshua said jumping up and offering her his stool.

"Where have you been?" he asked. "Why are you out of breath?" He searched for another stool for himself. Andrew and Galleon cast each other a smile.

"Oh, I've been out exploring. It's fascinating here. There are so many vines and bushes I've never seen before. We don't have anything like these where I'm from. I must have walked a mile or more but I really am quite hungry now. I normally eat early but none of you were up yet and, well, I didn't want to seem rude by eating before you. I am really very hungry now, though. What's for breakfast? I'm starving."

"FABLE? BREAKFAST! NOW!" Florelle shouted from behind the counter. She walked over to where they were sitting and said, "Breakfast will be with you in a mo', me darlings." She then disappeared through the door behind the counter with the still cooing Raetheon in her hand.

Before the door had a chance to close, Fable emerged through it with another steaming cauldron and brought it over. Joshua half expected him to throw it down in front of them and storm off, but instead he gently placed it on the table.

He brought them each a bowl and spoon and laid these out neatly on the table too. He ladled each bowl full with the steaming soup and looked at them each in turn.

"Eat yer Twiggling broth, then," he said, sneering at them with a scrunched-up face. "Yer'll be wanting a good breakfast inside before yer's head out again." With that, he nodded and left to tend to some of the other Traders.

"Blimey," Andrew said picking up a spoon and staring at the cauldron of broth. "He's in a good mood today."

"Good for him, at least," Galleon retorted. "That man has less charm than a Wood-boar that died of unnatural causes."

"You heard what Florelle said last night," Sarah scolded. "You'd be angry too if the only thing you knew for certain was how you were going to die."

Andrew and Galleon lowered their heads and tucked into the delicious Twiggling broth. Everyone had two more helpings, and the cauldron was all but empty by the time they had eaten their fill.

"Can you tell me more about the Goat?" Joshua asked Galleon.

"The Goat?" Sarah asked. "Who's that?"

"He's pure evil," Galleon grumbled. "He's an all-powerful, all-magical creature who likes to torment people for the sheer fun of it. Nobody knows where He comes from or where He hides, but He's said to have many magical powers. Within days, he wiped out my entire race."

Galleon peered glumly into his empty bowl. Before he could tell them anything more, Fable came back over to their table. To everyone's amazement, he dragged a stool over from the empty table next to them and took a seat.

"How's yer Twiggling broth?" he asked with a gruff tone.

"It was lovely," Sarah replied. "Were those Twiggling roots I could taste?"

Fable turned to frown at her. "Of course you could taste Twiggling roots," he said, raising his voice. "What else d'yer expect to find in Twiggling broth?"

He then looked over each shoulder before leaning in to say something. The others all leaned in too.

"I 'ear you are heading to the Valley of Moross," he whispered. "Reckon you'd like to know what yer future holds," he added in an even quieter voice, leaning in further. Checking once more over each shoulder, he pulled out from under his apron a bundle wrapped in cloth and laid on the table in front of him. They all leaned in some more and peered at it.

"What's that?" Joshua asked in a whisper.

Fable unwrapped the cloth to reveal a mirror. It was about the size of a hand, oval in shape with a short, wooden handle. Strange markings circled the edge.

"This 'ere…is the Mirror of Prophecy," Fable whispered.

"The Mirror of Prophecy?" Sarah belted out, sitting up straight.

"Shhhhhh!" Fable said waving his hand and holding a finger to his lips. One or two of the Traders on the far side of the inn glanced over before continuing with their broth. Joshua noticed the Trader with the cloak and hood again. He was still sitting in the dark corner with the same bowl of soup. Joshua wondered why he was eating so slowly. They all leaned in again.

"I'll let yer's 'av it," Fable whispered, sliding the mirror and bundle into the centre of the table.

"Why do you want to give it to us?" Joshua whispered back. Fable looked over his shoulders again to make sure nobody was listening.

"Look, this thing 'as brought me nothing but bleed'n misery. I'm pretty sure I'll be 'appier when it's gone."

"What makes you think it won't bring us misery too?" Andrew asked. Joshua turned to Fable and looked at him with raised brow.

"Don't look at it then," Fable suggested. "Maybe you can trade it for something valuable instead?"

The four of them all looked at each other. This seemed like a reasonable idea, Joshua thought. He didn't think there would be any harm in this, so he reached out and took the mirror. He wrapped the cloth around it again, then tucked it into his keeper bag.

All four of them stood up, leaving Fable sitting at the empty table. As they were making their way out, Andrew walked back over to Fable and whispered something in his ear. Fable got up, walked around to the back of the counter and dipped his hand into the jar of liquorice moss. He passed a handful of the treat to Andrew, who tucked it into his keeper bag before rejoining his friends.

CHAPTER NINE
Orb of Vision

The four companions had been walking for over an hour before Galleon insisted they stop and rest at a glade. Andrew paced the length of the clearing.

"How about some target practice? Come on. Let's see who can reach the highest point on that Yucust over there." He pointed to the tallest tree across glade. This one was taller than the one at Lake Morelle. Bunches of oval green leaves hung from the tree's trunks and protruded on either side.

"Are you sure you want to put yourself through this humiliation, Andrew?" Galleon asked. A smirk crept across his face.

"Well, if you don't think you're up to the challenge," Andrew chuckled, "feel free to bow out now. Don't worry, Sarah, I don't expect you to compete on our level."

Sarah lowered her head and peered at Andrew. A grin formed across her face and she put her hands on her hips. "OK, then, Andrew, show us all how it's done."

Joshua said nothing and watched with a smile to see how this would play out.

"Here, use these." Sarah reached into a nearby Bramock bush and rummaged around, plucking a few of the reddest berries.

"These are nice and hard. Here, take this one and show us just how good you are."

He took the hardened berry and placed it into the pouch of his slingshot.

Pulling back the pouch until the elastic vine was as taut as it could go, he aimed and launched the berry. It flew high across the glade and hit the tree near its base.

"Perfect." Andrew proclaimed with a smile. "That hit the tree square on," he went on, a smug look.

"I thought you said the object was to get as high into the tree as possible? I've vomited farther than that before. Come on. Move over and let me show you how it's done!" Galleon said, scratching his chin. He strutted over and gestured at both Andrew and Sarah to move aside.

"Let me have that slingshot, Andrew."

Andrew handed it over. Sarah plucked another Bramock berry, which she passed to Galleon.

The confident Imp stood there and took a deep breath, flexing his head side to side. He loaded the berry into the pouch, pulled it back and launched it into the air. It arced across the glade and hit the tree about half way up.

Andrew nodded and said, "Not bad."

"OK, can I have a go now?" Sarah asked. Andrew and Galleon glanced at each other. They both rolled their eyes and folded their arms.

"It's a powerful vine, this one. I made this slingshot myself," Andrew said, as he handed Sarah the slingshot. She studied the weapon and rubbed the stretchy vine between her fingers.

"That's what makes it go," Andrew said.

Sarah said nothing but kept feeling the vine along its length. She surveyed the flora around them. A nearby tree attracted her attention. It had several different types of vine dangling from one of its branches and she rolled all of them in turn between her fingers.

Andrew and Galleon glanced at each other again, this time with puzzled looks on their faces. After a while, Sarah pulled one of the vines and stripped it of its outer layer. Using both hands, she stretched its white inner core, folded it double and twisted it. She folded that double and twisted it again and then a third time.

Joshua just sat there smiling and waiting to see what she was up to.

She removed the vine from Andrew's slingshot and tossed it over her shoulder.

"Hey, it took me ages to break that in." Andrew protested.

Sarah ignored him and continued attaching the new vine. After pulling it back and forth a couple of times, she nodded and loaded a Bramock berry into the pouch.

Walking over to the exact spot where Andrew had stood, she cleared her throat as she lined up. With a single, swift motion, she pulled the pouch back and released the berry up into the air. It soared high into the sky and went clear over the top of the Yucust and landed somewhere out of sight.

Galleon and the two young men gawked at the tree with jaws dropped and eyebrows raised. All three of them looked at each other and then turned to stare at Sarah, who by now looked quite pleased with herself.

She giggled, shrugged her shoulders and passed Andrew's now improved slingshot back to him. He looked at it in disbelief.

"Where did you learn to do that?" Galleon and Andrew both asked together. Sarah just shrugged her shoulders again and grinned.

As she explained to Andrew and Galleon all about how vines have different elastic strengths, Joshua pulled out the Mirror of Prophecy from his keeper bag and unwrapped the cloth from around it.

The oval-shaped mirror was enclosed in a dark brown casing with a short handle. Cryptic markings sprawled around the rim. If it was writing, it was unlike anything Joshua had seen before. He held the mirror in his hand and peered into it.

As he looked and Sarah continued her explanation to the other two, his reflection faded and another blurry image filled the mirror. It was cloudy at first but the longer he looked, the more the image cleared, and his curiosity increased.

He could see a girl or young woman sitting on her knees, her head bent forward as if looking at the floor. She had her hands over her face.

As Joshua leaned forwards to look closer into the mirror, he could see she was crying. She was very upset. Seeing her in such pain was distressing. He felt powerless to help but continued to look closer to try and see who she was.

As the image sharpened, the girl lowered her hands to her knees, then looked up into the air and screamed in anguish. Tears rolled down her face. Joshua looked at her eyes and his heart stopped as the realisation hit him. It was Sarah, and she was crying as if heart-broken. Startled, Joshua threw the mirror to the ground and sprang to his feet.

"Are you OK?" Sarah asked. "You look like you've just seen a ghost."

The three of them stared at him.

"I'm...I'm fine. It's nothing. I...I just dropped the mirror, that's all."

Right at that moment, there was a rustle. It came from the woods behind them and they all spun around. They couldn't see anything, but Joshua sensed someone's presence, perhaps spying on them.

"Let's get moving again," he said. He bent down and picked up the mirror. Wrapping it in the cloth, he tucked it into his keeper bag.

"Come on," he said, and they all started walking across the glade, with Andrew and Galleon leading the way.

As they walked, Joshua, without turning his head, whispered to Sarah. "I think someone's following us."

Sarah nodded. She reached into her keeper bag and pulled out one of her Bramock berries. Unclipping her slingshot from her belt, she placed the hard fruit into its pouch and stretched it backwards as if aiming at the ground. Then she spun around and launched the projectile. It flew at great speed and struck the figure that was following them square in the head.

There was a groan as the figure dropped to its knees. Joshua, Andrew and Galleon turned, and they all ran back along the path to see who it was Sarah had struck.

Kneeling there was a dazed man dressed in a dark cloak. Joshua recognised him. It was the same man he had spotted sitting in the corner watching them this morning.

"Who are you, and why are you following us?" Joshua shouted at him.

Andrew had loaded his slingshot and was standing over the stranger with his weapon poised to shoot. The man roused and began rubbing his head.

"I mean you no harm," he groaned. He opened his eyes and peered up at the four of them standing over him. "You'll have no need for that," he gestured at Andrew's slingshot. "I'm not here to hurt you. My name is Melachor. I want to trade the mirror with you."

Joshua held his hand out to help the stranger up. Andrew kept his slingshot trained on him as he was helped to his feet.

"Do you normally skulk around in the forest spying on people like this?" Galleon chided.

"I'm sorry," Melachor replied. "I wanted to talk to you back at the inn but I didn't think it was safe. He has eyes everywhere. I had to be sure you weren't being followed first."

"Followed? By who? Whose eyes are everywhere?" Joshua demanded.

"The Goat's eyes, of course," Melachor shouted, rubbing his forehead. "Look, do you mind lowering your weapon?" he asked, flinching away from Andrew and holding his arm up to his face.

Joshua reached for Andrew's outstretched arm and pushed it down. Andrew looked at Joshua and slowly released the tension on his slingshot.

"The mirror!" Melachor demanded. "Where's the mirror? Do you still have it?"

"Why do you want the mirror so badly?" Joshua asked. "And what do you know of the Goat?"

Melachor stared at Joshua. He heaved a deep sigh and said, "My family was taken by the Goat. I've been searching for the Mirror of Prophecy for the last three years but with no luck. An old man told me the mirror will help me find them. I MUST have it!"

"Why would we give you the mirror?" Joshua asked.

"Because I have something you need. Something very valuable that will help you on your journey."

"What could you possibly have that's of value to us?" Galleon snorted.

Melachor looked down at the Imp. "You're an Imp?" Melachor asked. "The Goat wiped out your kind too. I know; I was there when it happened. My family were taken from me that day."

Galleon stared at Melachor. He was an imposing figure with a stocky build.

"Do you know if anyone escaped?" Galleon asked. "Were there any survivors?"

Joshua understood Galleon's urgency. He knew how he would feel if someone had information about his father's whereabouts.

"Survivors?" Melachor exclaimed, raising his brow. "Few people ever survive an encounter with the Goat. He's brutal. Nobody was spared that day, not even the women and children. Maybe a handful got away." He shook his head, and looked at the ground, "I don't know. I barely escaped with my own life. All I know is you should count yourself lucky to be alive, Imp."

"Seems convenient you escaped when so many didn't," Andrew scoffed.

Melachor stared at him. "I survived because of the orb," he said after a pause.

"What orb?" Joshua asked.

"Look, I don't really know much about it," Melachor hesitated. "All I know is that it helped me escape that day. It opened up some sort of portal or something. As I watched the Goat slaughtering people, I found a Trader that had the orb. He activated it somehow, and a vortex opened. I could see through it to the other side. It opened a tunnel through to another place. There were no people being killed on the other side, so I grabbed the orb and jumped through. My wife and children weren't so lucky.

Everything went dark after I entered the vortex, but when I next opened my eyes I found myself in a field outside a village near the Southern Tip. I was still clutching the orb when I came around. I don't know how long I was unconscious. If I didn't jump through to the other side, I would have been killed."

"Do you really expect us to believe that rubbish?" Andrew retorted, gripping the slingshot and tensioning the string again.

"It's the truth!" Melachor snapped, turning to sneer at him.

"What makes you think this orb of yours is any more valuable than the Mirror of Prophecy?" Joshua asked.

"I saw you looking into it earlier. You tell me," he said, with his hand held out.

Everyone else now turned to Joshua.

"You looked into the mirror?" Galleon asked with widened eyes. "What did you see?"

Joshua felt uncomfortable. He didn't know why he had seen Sarah so upset and didn't want to reveal this to anyone, least of all to Sarah. It would be cruel and unfair to her.

"I...I'm not sure what I saw. It probably doesn't mean anything anyway." He tried not to make eye contact with Sarah but he did notice Galleon was looking at him strangely. He wondered whether the Imp suspected him.

"Anyway, why would we have a need of your orb?" Joshua asked.

"You've looked into the mirror and have seen whatever it was prepared to reveal, so it has no more value to you, now. What I'm offering you is a way to transport yourself over great distances. If you can figure out how it works, surely that's worth more to you than a simple mirror?"

Joshua pondered this for a moment. On the surface, Melachor had a very good point. If the Mirror of Prophecy really had served its purpose, they would indeed have no further use for it. Perhaps the orb Melachor wanted to trade really would have more value.

He also thought about the misery the mirror had caused for Fable. Joshua was already second-guessing whether it was wise for him to have peered into the mirror. He regretted having seen that Sarah would someday experience such pain. That secret already felt like a burden.

He also worried one of the others might peer into the mirror if they held onto it any longer. Although knowledge of the future could be a good thing, the mirror had so far proven otherwise.

"OK, we'll trade you the mirror for the orb."

Melachor reached into his cloak and pulled out a roll of cloth. Joshua and the others leant in and stared at the spherical orb Melachor revealed. Joshua nodded to Melachor, who wrapped the orb again and handed it over.

Joshua reached into his keeper bag and pulled out the mirror, also still wrapped in cloth. With the exchange complete, Melachor walked back into the woods and was gone.

Joshua and the Magical Forest

CHAPTER TEN

The Romance Blossoms

"Are you sure that was wise?" Andrew said, turning to Joshua after Melachor was out of sight. "I mean, we don't know whether this orb really works or even how to use it."

Joshua tucked the orb into his keeper bag.

"Melachor was right. The mirror is useless to us now. Come on, let's get moving. Galleon, how much longer to the River of Torrents?"

"Probably another couple of days travel from here. The sooner we get going, the sooner we'll get there. Come on, Andrew and I will take point."

Galleon and Andrew went on ahead with Joshua and Sarah picking up the rear. Joshua was pleased to see them enjoying each other's company. They revelled in telling each other jokes and exchanging anecdotes about their different lives.

In contrast, Joshua and Sarah were very quiet. Joshua wanted to talk to Sarah but he was unsure of himself and didn't know what to say. After several minutes of awkward silence, Sarah spoke.

"Um, where are you from?"

Joshua was happy he had a chance to talk to Sarah on his own but he was unsure of himself. Clearing his throat bought him some time but didn't really know what he wanted to say. Mustering as much courage as he could, he forced himself to say something.

"Oh, um, well, I'm from a tribe over to the west," he said, finally managing to stumble the words out. "That is, the, um, well, it's the Morelle. I mean the Morelle tribe. I'm from the Morelle tribe." Joshua was kicking himself inside for having fumbled such a basic answer to an equally basic question. Sarah looked at him with a kind smile.

"Morelle," she slowly repeated. "I don't think I've been there, but the name does sound familiar for some reason."

"What about you? Where are you from? Originally, I mean," Joshua asked.

"Oh, I'm from the Far North," she said with a smile and another giggle. Each time she did this, Joshua's face beamed and he felt butterflies in his stomach. He loved that infectious little giggle. It was so cute.

She was innocent and resourceful, not to mention her aiming skills surpassed Andrew's. Beauty and skill; he'd never been so infatuated with anyone before and he was unsure how to react to these new and unfamiliar feelings.

"Have you ever heard of a place called Jemarrah?" she asked.

"Jemarrah? I know of it but I've never been there. I haven't seen much of Forestium. In fact, this is the farthest I've ever been from home."

"Really?" Joshua turned to her and their eyes met for the first time. They both looked ahead again, embarrassed. Then their eyes met again and both of them laughed at the same time.

The ice had broken between them. He had found his confidence and now felt he could talk to her more openly. As they walked, Joshua and Sarah told each other all about where they came from and the various adventures they had been on.

Joshua loved how Sarah laughed when he told her he originally wanted to be a Fixer. She told him she had been tinkering with things since she could crawl and always wanted to be a Fixer from as young as she could remember.

"It's customary in my tribe for Fixers to leave the village at the age of decision. The idea is to go exploring and to learn new things."

"You said you had been away for months. That's a long time to be away from home."

The two of them walked and talked for hours until the sun began casting long shadows.

"Let's make camp," Galleon suggested. "We've been walking for ages and I've got so many blisters, I'm practically walking on water. This clearing will do. We can stop here for the night."

"I'll find some Flame-bark," Sarah suggested.

"Flame-bark?" Joshua asked. He had never heard of it before. But he didn't care. Spending more time with Sarah made him feel warm inside, although he pretended to hide his enthusiasm.

"I'll go with you," he added. "I mean, if you want. I can help you carry it, if you want."

Sarah smiled and nodded. "Come on then. Let's see if we can find enough to keep the fire going all night."

Galleon and Andrew looked at each other and smiled, then set about removing the leaf-litter from the ground in the centre of the clearing. Joshua and Sarah went off in search of fuel for the night-fire, leaving the two of them to chat to each other.

"Joshua seems quite committed to finding his father. How long have you known him?"

"Ever since I can remember. We're practically brothers. He can be quite tenacious when he wants."

"Really? How so?" Galleon raised his brow.

"Well, he once tried to convince some of the village Fixers they were using the wrong wood to build wheels with. It was a few years ago. He would have been about twelve at the time."

"And were they?"

Andrew chuckled and shook his head.

"To prove his point, he found a piece of Ashfer wood and tried carving it into the shape of a wheel. He spent every waking hour on it night after night. Must have taken him a week before he was satisfied. When he finished, the Fixers attached the wheel to a cart and Joshua climbed on triumphantly."

"What happened?"

"They pushed it down the path. The wheel struck a rock and promptly broke in two. Sent him and the cart into a muddy ditch. I nearly wet myself laughing."

Galleon burst into laughter and said, "Some friend you are, Andrew."

"Don't fool yourself. There's nothing I wouldn't do for him. He's saved my life on more than one occasion."

By the time Joshua returned with Sarah some time later, they were each sporting a huge armfull of what looked like regular pieces of dried bark.

Meanwhile, Galleon had managed to get a small flame going. Sarah took some of her pieces of Flame-bark and threw them onto the fire one at a time. As each piece landed in the flame it ignited in a flash and burned intensely with a crackling sound. By the time all the Flame-bark was in place the fire was roaring fiercely and putting out lots of heat. Andrew stood there with his brow raised and mouth open.

"How did you know about this Flame-bark?" he asked Sarah as he took a seat beside the fire and enjoyed the warmth. "I've never seen such a small fire put out so much heat."

"Well, it was just a matter of experimenting with burning lots of different forest materials. I spent several days trying to see what worked best. Then I accidentally stumbled upon this particular type of bark. It was a few weeks ago when I was trying to figure out how to trap a Wood-boar. Wood-boars are attracted to heat, so I thought I'd see how to make better flames with more heat."

Andrew nodded and pursed his lips.

Joshua could see his best friend was starting to come around where Sarah was concerned. Andrew's initial misgivings and annoyances at her constant talking must be starting to give way to respect and admiration.

Joshua found himself wondering about how they were going to get across the River of Torrents. "You said something about Razorfins?" he asked Galleon.

"Hmmm," Galleon replied. "Nasty creatures, they are; very good swimmers and very large teeth. It's mating season, so the river will be full of them. A full-grown Razorfin would think nothing of ripping your arm or leg right off and coming back for seconds."

Andrew gulped and raised his eyebrow. There was a long pause as Galleon's words sunk in.

"Right, who's hungry?" Sarah said, smacking her hands together.

"I'm starving, but maybe we might try something other than boiled Shrooms tonight?" Galleon pleaded. "Maybe one of you can catch a couple of Chirvels?" he suggested, raising his eyebrows at Sarah.

"Come on then, Andrew. Let's see if we can put your improved slingshot to good use."

The two of them wandered off into the forest, leaving Joshua and Galleon sitting by the fire. After they were out of sight and out of earshot, Galleon got up and went to sit beside Joshua. He made himself comfortable and the pair sat there for a few minutes in silence enjoying the warmth of the crackling Flamebark. Eventually, Galleon turned to Joshua and asked him about what he saw in the Mirror of Prophecy.

"It was Sarah, wasn't it?" he whispered. "You saw Sarah in the mirror?"

Joshua looked at Galleon with surprise. "How could you possibly know that?"

"I didn't. At least not until your reaction just confirmed it."

Joshua's shoulders sank and he let out a sigh.

"You really like her, don't you? I can tell by the way you look at her. And do you know what? I'm pretty sure she likes you too."

Joshua blushed. His instinct was to shrug it off and deny it but he knew it was true. Galleon seemed to have a sixth sense about things, and Joshua didn't see any merit in pretending anymore.

Joshua paused for a moment before answering. "She was crying. I could see she was very upset. I mean really very upset, as if someone had died or something." He looked down at the ground and a tear started to well in his eye. "What does it mean? Why would she be so upset like that?"

"Well, I suppose you could ask the Oracle when we get to the Valley of Moross?"

Joshua pondered this. He wasn't sure he wanted to find out. At some point in the future Sarah would be deeply upset, and he'd rather not dwell on it. He also wondered whether he would be doing the right thing by telling her what he had seen. Besides, he was hoping the Oracle would help him find the truth about his dream and whether it was indeed his father he saw in great suffering. He wasn't even sure the Oracle would give him even that much information, let alone provide him with answers about Sarah's future.

"If you knew you were going to suffer in the future, would you want to know? What possible good could come from me telling Sarah what I saw?"

Galleon pondered this for a moment and said, "You're probably right. But I still think you should tell her about how you feel about her."

"How he feels about who?" Andrew said as he came walking back towards the fire with Sarah not far behind him. Joshua and Galleon stood up.

"Nothing. So, what's for dinner?"

"Delicious boiled Shrooms, of course," Sarah said laughing. She dropped the heap of Shrooms she was carrying onto the ground next to the fire. "Andrew *nearly* bagged a Chirvel."

"It wasn't my fault." Andrew quickly defended himself. "It is dark after all." They all laughed.

"Better practice your aim a bit more, Andrew," Galleon said with a chuckle, "unless you want to live off boiled Shrooms for the rest of the journey, that is."

They all settled in for the night. After boiling the Shrooms, Sarah collected a few other ingredients in the woods around the camp to spice up the food. Even Andrew commented on how much he liked this new recipe, and they all tucked in.

As the evening wore on everyone grew tired. The soothing humming sound of Dengles grew louder and this, along with the crackling of the Flame-bark on the fire, was making everyone drowsy. They each found a spot near the fire to lie down and got comfortable for the night.

Joshua cleared a spot next to Sarah and the two of them found comfort lying beside each other. As Sarah was just falling asleep, her arm fell next to Joshua's and their hands brushed against each other. Joshua felt a contented glow inside. Very gently, he extended his hand into Sarah's and they held hands. Joshua caught a smile spreading across Sarah's face as the two of them drifted off to sleep.

When Joshua awoke the following morning, he opened his eyes and found himself still lying next to Sarah with his arm clutched against her chest. Their hands were still entwined. Her gentle breathing and body warmth was soothing. Tenderly, he reached over and pushed her hair to one side to reveal the most beautiful face he'd ever seen.

Deciding to get up, he tried removing his hand. She inhaled deeply and Joshua froze for a second, but she settled again. Very carefully, he withdrew his arm, stood up and looked around.

Most of the Flame-bark had died down to coals and the early morning mist hung in the air. Chirvels were scurrying around nibbling at the scraps left over from last night's meal. There was a gentle rusting of leaves as the wind swayed the treetop canopy above them.

Andrew was on the far side of the fire and Galleon was curled up next to him in a ball, snoring away.

Sarah roused and opened her eyes. She stretched her arms, looked up at Joshua and smiled.

"Good morning," she whispered.

"Hi," he replied softly, smiling down at her. "Did you sleep well?"

Sarah smiled and nodded. He offered his hand to help her up. She took it and got to her feet. The two of them stood there in the still morning air, face to face, still clutching each other's hands.

Joshua's heart raced as they stared at each other. Neither of them spoke, but they both smiled. Joshua felt the same butterfly sensation welling in his stomach again. It happened each time their eyes met or whenever he got close to her.

Sarah gently tightened her grip on his hand. Mesmerised, he moved his head forward just a little, still gazing into her deep blue eyes. She moved her head closer in response. Full of expectation, they leaned towards each other.

"Hey, what's for breakfast?" Andrew blurted out, giving a loud yawn from the other side of the fire. Sarah released Joshua's hand and the two of them broke eye contact and backed away from each other.

Sarah walked around the fire and busied herself collecting some twigs and throwing them onto the dying coals, which burst into flames. Joshua's heart was still racing. He felt embarrassed and looked around to find something to occupy himself. Noticing Galleon was still snoring, he decided this would be an appropriate distraction and went over to nudge him.

The slumbering Imp woke with a shock and looked around before taking in the fact it was Joshua standing over him. Relaxing, he pushed himself to his feet, yawned and stretched.

"Right then, we've got a good day's travel ahead of us if we're to reach the River of Torrents before dark, so we'd better make an early start. We can find something to eat along the way."

Sarah collected their things, and Andrew stamped out the fire. They set off in the direction of the rising sun. Once more, Andrew and Galleon walked ahead. They told each other jokes and, once again, Joshua and Sarah were quiet. After an hour, Sarah was the first to break the silence.

"You really loved your father, didn't you, Joshua?" she said in a tender voice, casting him a sideways glance. Joshua looked at her, puzzled.

"Why do you say that?" He hadn't yet told Sarah the reason he was making his way to the Valley of Moross was to seek guidance from the Oracle about his father.

"Well…it's just…"

"Go on," Joshua asked, smiling, "just…what?"

"Well, you talk in your sleep," Sarah giggled. It gave him that same warm sensation inside again and he smiled. "What happened to him?" she asked.

"I don't know," Joshua replied, shaking his head after a long pause. "He left when I was very young. I saw him recently in a dream. Well, at least I think it was him. The person I saw was in great pain. So much pain." Joshua stared into nothingness, trying to understand the meaning of it all. "The reason we're going to the Valley of Moross is because my village Elder told me to seek the advice of the Oracle there."

Sarah nodded, but didn't say anything.

"What about you? What are your parents like?" Joshua asked, snapping himself back to reality.

"Oh, well, I never actually knew my mother. She died when I was very young. Dad's a Warrior." She rolled her eyes and smiled. "Well, at least he used to be a Warrior when I was younger, I mean. He's the village Elder now. Fortunately, there haven't been any wars with other tribes for many years. It's so much better now that Forestium is a peaceful place, don't you think?"

Joshua smiled and nodded.

"It was horrible whenever he went off to battle; I used to hate it. I'd often cry myself to sleep when he was away." She looked at the ground and shook her head slowly. "I used to worry he wouldn't come back."

"Sounds like you really love your father too."

"Hmm, very much so. I can understand how you feel about wanting to know what happened to your father. In some ways, you remind me of my father."

Joshua looked at her again and asked, "Really? In what way?"

"Well, you're single-minded, determined and strong, for one thing, but at the same time, you're very tender and sweet." She giggled again. This time it was a more relaxed giggle.

Sarah looked Joshua in the eye and said. "I really love my father."

Joshua nodded and smiled.

"Of course, you're also very different from him in many ways too. For one thing…"

"Yes?" He cast her another sideways glance.

"You're also…well…very cute."

The two of them stopped walking and looked at each other again. Joshua sensed that warm feeling inside his stomach and his heart raced. Everything about Sarah was intoxicating. He loved the way she smiled and looked him in the eye. She was beautiful, resourceful, intelligent and tender.

Reaching up, he gently moved a few strands of her hair from her eyes. As he moved the hair aside, his hand caressed her cheek and she smiled. Her eyes widened, and Joshua began losing himself in the moment. They slowly moved closer. Everything around them faded, and Joshua felt his insides tumbling with anticipation as they closed their eyes.

"Hey, look! I can see the river" Andrew shouted at them from ahead. "Oh, um, never mind," he said, turning back again, pretending he did not notice the two of them were very likely on the verge of kissing.

They both laughed.

"Come on," Sarah said. "Let's go see what this river looks like."

The two of them caught up with Andrew and Galleon.

"Thanks." Joshua whispered to Andrew, casting him a sideways glance. The sarcasm was not lost on Andrew, who silently mouthed the word 'sorry'.

Joshua and the Magical Forest

CHAPTER ELEVEN

Crossing the River

The murky, brown river was raging with white crests up and down its length. It formed a natural boundary to the forest they had just emerged from. There were very few trees on the other side of the river, marking a distinct change in scenery. This was the first time Joshua had seen anything other than forest terrain.

In this part of Forestium wooded forests give way to rolling fields that in turn led to a crescent-shaped range of mountains. These marked the far eastern boundary of Forestium. The majestic, snow-peaked mountaintops could be clearly seen from here.

"How are we going to get across that?" Andrew asked, pointing at the turbulent waters. Shielding his eyes from the sun, he stared at the distant riverbank.

Galleon squinted and said, "It doesn't look that far to the other side but there's no way we can swim across."

Unclipping his slingshot, Andrew found a pebble by the water's edge. He loaded it into the pouch and launched it to the far side of the river.

"No, no way," he agreed, shaking his head and staring at where pebble had landed.

"Not that you'd want to try anyway. You'd be dragged under by Razorfins long before you made it half way across, assuming you were a good enough swimmer to get even that far to begin with. You'd be stripped to bare bone before you got to the other side." Galleon walked over to Joshua.

"Do you see where the mountain range starts over there?" Galleon pointed towards where the rocky summits began off to their right. Joshua could just about make out where the white-tipped peaks emerged from the clouds.

"That's the entrance to the Valley of Moross. The valley is formed between the mountains that you can see and another range of mountains right behind them. The crescent-shaped valley runs between the two."

As they all peered into the distance, a huge silvery creature about half their size with a long row of sharp teeth launched itself out of the water in front of them. It thrashed several times from side to side before landing with a huge splash. Andrew took several steps back from the water's edge. He turned and looked at the others with his jaw dropped.

"Told you Razorfins were nasty creatures," Galleon snorted. "Their teeth are like shards of flint. If one of those bites you, it'll rip the flesh right off your arm."

"Isn't there a way around?" Andrew pleaded.

"Well," Galleon pointed south, "that way leads out to sea. It's several weeks travel to the north," he indicated in the other direction, "before the river narrows. Every step we take from here is another step we'll have to take back again to get as close as we are now to the entrance to the valley."

"We can cross here," Sarah pointed at the river. The other three turned and looked at her.

"Um, I don't know if you noticed but there are huge creatures with huge teeth and probably huge appetites lurking in those waters," Andrew said, pointing to where the large Razorfin had just appeared. "You did see that vicious beast that just launched out of the water, didn't you?"

"I don't mean we should swim across. We probably won't need to get wet at all," she said, studying one of the trees on the far side of the riverbank.

"Um, probably?" Andrew asked, raising his eyebrows and shaking his head.

"Perhaps we could fell a tree?" Galleon suggested. "It might just reach to the other side and we could just walk across. Andrew could lead the way, of course."

Sarah glanced around. She examined the trees on their side of the riverbank in turn. She surveyed each tree one by one, and then turned her attention to a tree on the far side, before appearing to reach some sort of conclusion.

"Hmmm," she said, tapping her lips with her finger. "I think," she pondered for a moment. "Yes," she declared. "Wait here for a minute!"

Without another word, she walked straight back into the forest. Galleon, Joshua and Andrew all shrugged their shoulders and looked at each other. They each wondered what the industrious young woman had in mind.

Nearly half an hour passed, and Joshua was starting to worry where she was, when she emerged to find the three of them sitting by the water's edge. Andrew had chosen a spot farthest away from the riverbank and was keeping a keen eye out for more Razorfins.

She carried what looked like several lengths of vine, which she threw to the ground.

"What are we going to do with all this?" Andrew asked. His tone was no longer sarcastic.

"This is what we're going to use to get across the river," Sarah said. She bent down and picked up a length of the vine. "Here," she handed it to Andrew. "See if you can pull this until it breaks." Andrew took the vine and grabbed a piece with both hands and started pulling. To his astonishment, he wasn't able to pull the vine to breaking point.

"OK, so how are we going to use this to get us across the river?" Joshua asked, getting to his feet.

Sarah continued to concentrate on what she was doing. She secured a length of Ashfer wood to the end of the vine. She untangled the remainder and laid it out up and down the riverbank, taking care not to entangle it. Unclipping her slingshot, she loaded the knotted Ashfer into the pouch. She pulled back hard on the slingshot and aimed it at the tree on the far side of the river. The piece of wood with vine attached flew across the river. As it did, it dragged the carefully laid out vine with it, making a swishing sound as the vine was taken up off the riverbank.

103

The projectile dropped between two branches of the distant tree. Sarah pulled back hard on the vine and it snagged itself securely.

Andrew, Joshua and Galleon stood there, dumbfounded. It became clear just what Sarah was up to.

Andrew began inspecting the trees around them. He pointed to one particular branch. "This one here?"

"You're a quick learner, Andrew. OK, do you think you can hook this end over that branch?"

Andrew smiled at her and nodded. He took his slingshot, tied a pebble to the end of the vine and launched it towards the branch. It looped over the sturdy limb on the first shot and the pebble landed on the ground next to him. He pulled on the vine and tied it off to the base of the tree with a secure knot. It was now taut across the river between the two trees.

"We're not done yet. We'll never make it across with just our bare hands to support our weight."

She took another long piece of vine and threw it over the top of the horizontal vine and tied it off in a loop at one end. Andrew, who was perhaps the heaviest of the four, stood onto the loop that was now suspended over the taut line. He bounced up and down a few times to test its strength.

Even with his full weight, there was still plenty of clearance above the surface of the choppy water.

"This seems strong enough. I'll go first."

With both hands on the taut horizontal line and using the loop to support most of his weight, he manoeuvred himself across the river. Shuffling sideways, he made his way over and jumped to the riverbank when he reached the other side. With the loop now free of Andrew's weight, Sarah pulled it back to their side again.

"Right, you next," Joshua gestured to Galleon.

"Me? OK, but if I fall in and die, I'm going to kill you for this." The Imp repeated the same process and made his way to the other side of the river. Once he was on the far side, Sarah pulled the loop back again and made her own way across.

With Sarah also safely over it was Joshua's turn.

He made it half-way across the roaring torrent when the taut vine from which he was dangling dropped, leaving him hanging just above the water. He looked back to see the vine unravelling where it had frayed against a branch. Splashes of the raging rapids beneath him were reaching his feet.

Trying not to panic, he continued to inch his way across. Then a huge Razorfin jumped out of the water and thrashed about right next to him. Joshua panicked and lost his footing on the loop as the unravelling vine dropped him even lower.

Hanging on for dear life, he dangled with both feet in the water up to his ankles. He tried to lift his feet but he struggled against his own body weight, causing the vine to tear into the flesh of his fingers. Joshua's face contorted as he tried frantically to keep himself out of the water.

The vine unravelled some more, and Joshua sank further into the freezing cold, Razorfin-infested river. The fast-moving water frothed all around him. The force of the water was so great that it was pulling on him, making it even more difficult to maintain his grip.

A frenzy of blood-thirsty Razorfins snapped around him and splashed near the surface. Then the line went completely slack. Joshua found himself immersed in the freezing water, carried along by the strong current.

Struggling to keep his head above the turbulence, he tumbled this way and that, thrashing his arms about in vain. He somehow managed to find the vine and grabbed hold of it.

The bitterly cold waters sapped his strength, and he was no longer sure of which way was up. He felt the vine tighten; he clung to it with all his might.

A Razorfin brushed against him as he took a gulp of air only to find his mouth full of water. Spluttering and coughing, he took in a second gulp of the murky, brown liquid as he continued to grip the vine for dear life and struggled to find the surface of the water.

As his head went under again, he could sense another huge Razorfin brush against him. It raced towards him and Joshua felt the beast's powerful tail thrash against him. He managed to get his head above water to take a gasping breath but the strong current pulled him under again. He feared he might pass out from being unable to breathe as he tried to reach for the surface of the water.

Suddenly, with a frenzy of Razorfins all around him, something grabbed his arm and tugged. It pulled hard, and the next minute Joshua found himself landing on the riverbank with Andrew holding on to one of his arms, dragging him away from the water's edge. Andrew collapsed beside him and Sarah rushed over.

"Joshua? Are you all right?" she cried, cradling his head. Joshua opened his eyes and coughed out a mouthful of water. He took a deep gasp of breath and felt the life slowly returning to him. After several more panting breaths he sat up and looked at the raging water from which his friends had just rescued him.

"I'm fine," he said, wiping the water from his face. Sarah flung her arms around him and cried. Joshua hugged her tightly.

"I'm fine," he repeated. "It's all over. I'm safe now." Sarah's embrace lingered as she continued to cry. Gradually, her sobs subsided.

CHAPTER TWELVE

Valley of Moross

After they had recovered from their ordeal, the four travellers set out towards the mountain range and the entrance to the Valley of Moross.

"I hope it won't take too long to find the Oracle when we get there," Joshua said to Andrew.

"Whatever happens, I think you've already found something worth the journey." Andrew gestured to Sarah, who was walking with Galleon up ahead. Joshua smiled and nodded.

"It's good to see you so relaxed. I really thought you were done for when you dropped into the river back there."

"I guess I have you to thank for the fact I'm still here."

"Don't worry," Andrew nudged his friend, "I won't let you forget it."

"Won't let him forget what?" Galleon asked.

"Saving his life back there."

"Well, just keep on your toes, Andrew. We might all need your services when we get to the valley."

"Do you think you'll find any Imps there?" Andrew asked.

Galleon heaved a deep sigh. "I don't know. Maybe. One way or another, something tells me we should all keep on our toes. Whoever lives in that valley might be a bunch of cannibals for all we know."

Everyone paused and pondered Galleon's words.

"Well, I for one am looking forward to it." Sarah said, breaking the awkward silence. "I can't wait to see what I can learn there."

None of them had been to this part of Forestium before. As they got closer to the valley, Joshua found he was becoming more anxious about what they might find there. Sarah was loving every minute of it. She bristled with enthusiasm for all the new things they might discover and what new skills she could acquire.

Travelling across the rolling, windswept hills was unlike travelling through forest and woodland. Patches of fog drifted over the plains, invoking a sense of isolation. From time to time, the wind would pick up and sweep the mist away to reveal the imposing mountain peaks getting closer day by day.

The lack of trees allowed Sarah the opportunity to be even more inventive with finding ingredients for cooking meals. There were no Chirvels, Wood-boars or any of the other more familiar forest creatures they would typically hunt.

The exposed terrain meant finding shelter was also difficult. Keeping warm meant huddling up together during the cool nights. Joshua and Sarah didn't mind so much, as it gave them all the more reason to get close to each other.

Each night, Andrew and Sarah would head out to hunt wild grassland Flarrets, whilst Joshua and Galleon prepared the fire. Although nimble, the small, furry animals could only run in short bursts. They were skittish and only came out of their burrows when they felt safe.

Andrew took to crouching behind the entrance to the Flarret holes but each time one of the brown and white beasts came out far enough it would duck back in again as soon as it sensed his presence.

Sarah's technique of setting traps using nothing more than small loops of vine and a few rocks was much more successful, not to mention far less effort. Each evening she would return with at least three of the meaty Flarrets strung over her shoulder and Andrew with none. It was a constant source of amusement around the campfire but Andrew didn't seem to mind. He just laughed along with everyone else.

With so few food options, everyone was glad to have real meat to eat instead of the bland grass seeds, which for the most part were the only other food available. None of them found the small, yellowish Shrooms that grew across the grasslands to be appealing. A fully grown wild Flarret, however, would make a decent meal for two people.

After several days of travelling across the plains they reached the entrance to the Valley of Moross. The valley floor was formed between the peaks of the two adjacent mountain ranges towering on either side.

Nobody spoke much. Joshua felt a tension in the air. He had an eerie feeling someone was already here, watching them, possibly even waiting for them. He couldn't quite put his finger on it. Galleon noticed several black flags, flapping in the wind part-way up the mountain foothills on either side of the valley entrance.

"What do you suppose those are?" Andrew asked as they got closer to the flags.

"I don't know," Galleon answered, shaking his head. "They don't look like tribal flags. I can't make out the emblem." He squinted at the marks emblazoned on each of the black flags. "It looks like…" he paused and lowered his brow, "it looks like horns…yes, two horns."

Joshua had a sinking feeling it might be a warning of some kind. Perhaps someone or something didn't want people entering the valley. He stopped short of voicing this concern for fear of putting everyone on edge any more than they already were. By the look on his face, Joshua thought Galleon had come to a similar conclusion.

Not long after passing through the valley entrance they saw the first sign of human habitation since leaving Fable and Florelle's inn. From a distance, it looked like a cluster of huts at the base of the foothills.

Winding footpaths led away from the huts in several directions but there was nobody around: no animals, no movement of any kind. The rustling wind carried smoke from many fires, so they decided to take a closer look.

As they approached, their jaws dropped. Everyone stood there with wide eyes.

"What happened here?" Joshua murmured in wonder.

"I don't know," Galleon replied, "but whoever did this, they certainly were thorough. This place has less charm than Fable."

"Doesn't look like a single building has been left untouched." Andrew said. He walked on ahead to get a better look.

"Who would have done such a horrible thing?" Sarah asked, her hand held to her mouth.

"No idea, but judging by the smoke, it must have happened recently," Joshua said.

All of the buildings were in complete ruin. Roofs were missing and everything was charred. Implemented and belongings were spread around disarray. It looked like an army of marauders had swept through and torn the village apart.

"There's nobody here! Not a single body!" Andrew shouted back at them.

Joshua surveyed the scene in silence, trying to figure out what might have happened. He was hoping to find a clue: anything that might explain the scene of total devastation before them.

"Warring tribes?" Galleon suggested, turning to Joshua.

"I don't think so," Sarah said, as she too looked around to take in as much as she could. "It can't be. There would be survivors, or at least bodies. And besides, there haven't been tribal wars in Forestium for years."

"Maybe not from where we come from but it might be different here." Joshua said. "For all we know, they could all be at war with each other."

"Hmmm. That's true. I wonder what happened to everyone. This was clearly once a living village and not that long ago."

"Well, if it was a tribal war, there should at least be bodies. It doesn't make any sense."

They pressed on through the valley with the foothills of the mountains on either side. Making their way slowly through the crescent-shaped valley floor, they encountered more settlements, all of which exhibited the same scene of total devastation. Most of the buildings had been burned to the ground, and not a soul, living or dead, was anywhere to be found.

"What could have done this?" Andrew said, gaping at the burned remnants of the buildings.

"The Goat," Galleon exclaimed after a long and reflective pause. "This is what happened when my people were taken. I'll bet you anything this is His doing. Those flags we saw before must be the Goat's mark."

Joshua felt a weird sensation as they continued through the valley. It became more noticeable with each step.

"What's that strange noise?" Andrew asked.

"I can hear it too," Galleon said. "It started a few minutes ago, and I think it's getting louder."

"I can't hear where it's coming from," Sarah added. They all looked around to try to find the source of the noise.

"Joshua, it's you!" she said.

Joshua looked down at his keeper bag. He felt a strange vibration coming from it. He reached in and took out the orb. As he unwrapped the cloth, he could see a faint glow around the orb, which continued its quiet humming.

The clear, spherical crystal had an engraving of an eye on one side, and this was where the glow was coming from. As he moved around with the orb, the humming grew louder and then softer, and the eye glowed brighter and then dimmer. It seemed to change depending on which direction he was facing.

"It's a beacon!" Sarah exclaimed with wide eyes.

Joshua circled. The orb vibrated and glowed more when he pointed it north through the valley, so they carried on in that direction. It acted as a compass and led them to a rocky outcrop part way up the foothills on the eastern side, about half way through the valley.

Using the orb to guide him, Joshua located a secluded entrance to a cave. It was surrounded by huge boulders and thick vegetation and they had to squeeze to get through the narrow opening.

Once inside, the orb began pulsating rapidly. It glowed so brightly the path ahead of them was illuminated enough to allow them to venture deeper into the cave. The winding passage narrowed as the orb led them through a labyrinth of twists and turns.

Joshua could see his breath through the chilly air each time he exhaled. They continued until they could no longer see the daylight from the entrance. Now they were totally dependent on the orb and its glow.

Without warning the orb stopped vibrating and the glow dimmed and went out altogether, plunging them into darkness. Sarah reached for Joshua's hand and squeezed it tightly.

The sudden darkness gave them a fright, but Joshua's eyes adjusted and it became clear there was still a faint flicker of light coming from somewhere. He looked around to try to find the source of the glow. It came from just around a corner ahead of them.

Turning a corner, they entered a cavern and found the source of the light. It was a small, blue flame, no bigger than a fist, in the centre of the cavern. It hovered above the ground at about waist height and cast eerie shadows on the walls around them.

Joshua was puzzled at how the flame sustained itself, as there was no wood or other material visible. The ground beneath the flame was flat and empty. Encircling it was a ring of stones.

Joshua made his way around them to see what else was in the cavern, but there was nothing other than the flame. He carefully stepped over the ring of stones to get closer to the flame. He reached out with one hand, but he couldn't feel any heat coming from it.

Just then, the flame erupted and filled half the cavern. It shot high up into the ceiling that seemed to go on forever. It was so bright that everyone recoiled and turned their heads away.

CHAPTER THIRTEEN

Oracle of Forestium

After a few seconds, the flame died down about half way. Small sparks were emanating from the top of the flame and floating up into the air. Just as Joshua's eyes adjusted to the new level of brightness, a voice echoed around the cave.

"The pure of heart may command the flame, for he is worthy that the Oracle may assist…"

The soft voice seemed to come from within the flame itself. It was reassuring, with a high pitch like that of a young woman. As each word was spoken, blue sparks erupted and flew into the air, trailed by wisps of smoke. Joshua looked into the flame with wide eyes and pondered the cryptic words.

"Are, are you the…um…are you the Oracle?" he asked, trying not to fumble his words. Joshua's heart raced. There was a pause before the Oracle spoke.

"I am the one, the source. The answers you seek lie here within…"

Joshua recoiled at the sudden sound. He looked at the others before squinting at the flame.

"I…I want to know who it was I saw in my dream. Was it my father? Is he alive?"

Again, there was a pause before the Oracle spoke and Joshua waited with bated breath.

"The truths you seek are not easily foretold. Visions of suffering cloud your future, young Joshua. Are you prepared to pay the price that answers may be granted to the knowledge you seek?"

Joshua didn't understand what the Oracle was saying. Did the answers come at a price? He was willing to pay a price for the knowledge the Oracle had, but why did it have to be so cryptic? Why couldn't the Oracle just come out and say whatever it was that needed to be said?

"Um, price?" Joshua asked, peering into the flame with his brow raised and his head tilted forward.

The Oracle continued to speak in a sweet tone, "You are worthy of heart, Joshua, but your path will be a difficult one. To learn what you seek, you must accept your destiny. Are you prepared to pay the price?"

This puzzled Joshua. He hadn't bargained on having to give anything in exchange for the information he sought. He pursed his lips and thought for a moment.

"I am prepared," the nervous young man replied, still gazing into the Oracle's orange flame. In truth, Joshua wasn't prepared at all but he desperately wanted to hear what the Oracle had to say next. He raised his hands to his mouth and tensed his shoulders waiting for the Oracle to respond.

There was a blinding flash, and he found himself engulfed entirely within the flame, levitating above the ground. He felt disconnected from reality. The flame was no longer moving but was all around him and he couldn't feel any heat. He was aware of his friends standing around the circle of stones but they weren't moving either. The sensation was strangely comforting. He felt safe. It was as if time had stopped.

Just as he was adjusting to this new reality, the Oracle spoke. It was the same gentle voice but it was somehow different. Instead of the sound echoing around the cavern, this time it came from within his own mind.

"The Orb of Vision that brought you to me is but one of three magical orbs that exist in this world, Joshua. The Orb of Time lies within this cave. You will find the Orb of Suffering guarded by the Elder of the northernmost village of Forestium. Bring the three orbs together to open the Portallas. Your father awaits you on the other side."

"But beware, Joshua. You must bring the orbs together with haste, for you are not the only one to seek their power. The one who banished my children also seeks the power. The love you have found cannot last, Joshua. The knowledge of this is the price you must pay."

There was another bright flash and Joshua found himself once again standing in the cavern with the others. The flame died down to its original size and was again a flickering with a blue hue. Beneath it now lay a roll of cloth. Joshua reached down and picked it up. He unrolled it to find another orb inside. This crystal had a carving of an hourglass engraved into it on one side, but was otherwise was exactly the same as the Orb of Vision.

"The Orb of Time," Joshua whispered as he gazed at the orb.

"Um, the orb of what?" Andrew asked. "How did that get there?"

Joshua turned and looked at the other three.

"I just spoke with the Oracle."

"Yes, we heard," Andrew said, "you told it you were prepared to hear what it had to say."

"No, you don't understand. I was in the flame. I heard the Oracle's voice inside my head."

Andrew and Galleon looked at each other with raised brows and pursed lips.

"What did the Oracle say to you?" Sarah asked. She at least seemed ready to accept Joshua's account of what he had just experienced. Joshua paced back and forth, staring at the ground.

"She said I had to find the third orb, the Orb of Suffering. I think that's what she said called it. She said the Elder in the northernmost village of Forestium was looking after it and that I should bring the three orbs together to open something called a Portallas. She said my father was on the other side."

"What was all that stuff about paying the price, then?" Galleon asked. "What's the price you have to pay for this information?"

Joshua thought about this and his heart sank. He caught Sarah's eye. The Oracle had told him the love he had found could not last. Was the Oracle talking about his love for Sarah?

"I...I don't know," Joshua broke eye contact with Sarah. "It was all a bit cryptic. I...I'm just not sure. She said we had to be quick, though. Something about the one responsible for banishing her children was also trying to get the orbs. She said we had to get the three orbs before he did or the Portallas thing wouldn't work and I'd lose my father forever."

"The one who banished her children? What's that all about?" Andrew asked.

"I don't know. Maybe she means the one that's responsible for all the people in the valley who have gone missing?"

"Hang on! Did you say the northernmost village?" Sarah asked, narrowing her eyes and tilting her head.

"Yes, why?"

"Well, that could very well be my village, Jemarrah. It's in the far north and might even be the most northern village in all of Forestium."

"Hang on a minute! Didn't you say your father was the Jemarrah village Elder?"

"Yes, that's right."

"That's him! That's who the Oracle said was guarding the Orb of Suffering. That's where we have to go next!"

Christopher D. Morgan

CHAPTER FOURTEEN
The Goat

Melachor had made it back to his secluded hut deep in the forest. He waited for several days to make sure he was not followed before attempting to gaze into the Mirror of Prophecy. He desperately wanted to use the mirror in the hope of learning what had happened to his family but he was also nervous the Goat might have spies everywhere. Having waited for years to get his hands on the mirror, he wasn't about to take any chances now it was finally in his possession. The mirror, he hoped, would lead him to his family, and he would protect it from the Goat at all costs. Waiting a few days just to be sure seemed like a small price to pay to get to see what happened to his wife and children.

On this dark and cool night, when swarms of Dengles drowned out the noise of the wind rushing through the forest canopy, he took the bundle of cloth from beneath the floorboards where he had hidden it. Unwrapping it, he removed the mirror, raised it up to his face and peered in.

The image of his reflection swirled, gradually fading away. A murky image replaced it. Melachor leaned forward to get a better look.

Then, without warning, a hand reached through the mirror and violently grabbed him by the throat.

It lifted him off his knees and gripped with such strength he could no longer breathe. The mirror floated in mid-air with Melachor dangling from the end of the Goat's protruding arm. He grabbed at the Goat's wrist with both hands and frantically tried to free himself from the vice-like grip, but it was no use. He felt himself being pulled through the mirror.

The Goat's grotesque face stared at him. It was crowned with two ribbed, black horns that curled out from either side of his head. The hideous creature peered up at him from under a thick, bushy brow. Melachor could make out the whites beneath the Goat's glistening, black eyes. An untidy white tuft of hair hung from beneath His chin. The grip the Goat had on Melachor's throat was excruciating, and he felt he was going to pass out as he thrashed his feet about, trying to find a solid surface beneath them.

There was an almighty roar as the Goat screamed into Melachor's face. The horrific sound reverberated around his head. His body and legs went limp and dangled lifelessly beneath him. Just as he thought he was about to die, the Goat released his grip and Melachor dropped to the floor in a heap.

With his windpipe open again, Melachor gasped. His eyes were still closed as he desperately tried to inhale some life-giving air.

The Goat strutted around the gasping man, lying curled in a ball on the floor in total confusion. He was still writhing in agony, coughing and spluttering.

"You DARE to use MY magical power?" the Goat roared down at His captive, His hairy arms protruding from either side of his muscular torso, his fists clenched. He thrashed his head from side to side and roared again.

"Please," Melachor pleaded sobbing uncontrollably, trying to take more breaths, "have mercy on me, please."

"Why did you just use the mirror?" the Goat demanded. He kicked Melachor with one of his hooves. Although Melachor was not a small man, this blow sent him flying across the floor and he landed several paces away face down, clutching at his stomach.

The Goat stared at him as He paced back and forth. Each time He turned, He kept his gaze fixed on the whimpering man across the room.

"I could kill you now, worthless wretch. Maybe I will and maybe I won't. Please me and I will consider letting you live. Now, I will ask you again. Why did you DARE use the mirror?"

He paced up and down, waiting for Melachor to respond to his question.

"I grow tired of hearing my voice alone, but I will ask you one more time, impudent wretch, why did you DARE to use the Mirror of Prophecy?"

Melachor caught his breath and surveyed his surroundings. It was dark and musky, and he couldn't see any features of the room other than the Goat pacing up and down. He couldn't sense anyone else present and the only sound was the clicking of the Goat's hooves.

"WELL?" the malevolent brute demanded.

"Please," Melachor begged, "I only wanted to find my family. I want to know if they are safe."

"Hmm. I've tolerated people using the mirror for far too long. How did you come by it?" the Goat bellowed. His voice seemed calmer but He was still a terrifying figure. His initial rage had subsided and His pacing slowed.

"I…I traded it," Melachor replied with teary eyes. "I exchanged it for an orb."

The Goat stopped pacing altogether.

"Orb?" The Goat shook his head violently and peered around the room. "Tell me about this orb!"

"It opened up a gateway," Melachor said. He had caught his breath somewhat and was sitting upright but was still cowering in fear. "I escaped through the gateway many years ago when you destroyed the Imps."

The Goat looked Melachor in the eye, then roared.

"You mean the Orb of Vision. Where is it? Tell me, NOW!"

"I…I don't know where it is, I swear." Melachor whimpered, "I told you, I traded it with a group of travellers. I think they were heading for the Valley."

Melachor's bottom lip quivered as he cowered on the floor.

"If…if I knew where the orb was, I…I'd tell you. Please. I'll do anything. Just…don't kill me."

The Goat looked up and started pacing back and forth again. His eyes darted around and He growled. Melachor felt glad the

Goat was, at least for now, preoccupied with the orb and its whereabouts.

The Goat stopped pacing and turned to look at Melachor again.

"Tell me about these travellers! Who are they?"

"I don't know who they are," Melachor whimpered. "I just traded the mirror with them. A young Woodsman with a couple of companions, I think. An Imp was travelling with them."

The Goat mumbled to himself. "Hmmm. The Orb of Time lies hidden with the Oracle. He must not find it…"

He let out a grunt and stomped towards Melachor, who raised his hand to his face and turned his head away in fear.

"You lie. There are no Imps in Forestium. I banished them all from that realm. I should kill you now for your impudence."

The Goat raised his arm as if to strike a blow.

"No, I…I swear it's the truth," Melachor cried.

The Goat peered down at him, looking the petrified man directly in the eye. The Goat's dark eyes and imposing silhouette were a terrifying sight. Slowly, the Goat lowered His arm to His side. He turned and resumed His pacing again, all the while mumbling to himself.

"I must find the orbs," the Goat murmured, peering around the dark room. "If the three orbs come together before…"

He turned to Melachor again and said, "I will send my scouts to find them."

With that, He clapped several times, looked up and howled. Within seconds, Melachor could hear what he thought might be huge bats flying around high above them in the depths of the dark ceiling. Whatever the creatures were, they flew around for several seconds before the flapping sound faded away.

Christopher D. Morgan

CHAPTER FIFTEEN
Blood-bats

Joshua and the others tracked north through the Valley of Moross. Joshua was replaying his encounter with the Oracle over and over in his mind. Although it was very clear what he needed to do, he was troubled by what the Oracle had said about his love for Sarah. He kept repeating it in his mind.

"The love you have found cannot last, Joshua. The knowledge of this is the price you must pay."

"Why?" he thought to himself. It seemed so unfair. Sarah was the best thing to happen to him in a long time, and he had just started to explore his stirring feelings for her. Would he have to give this all up? The thought both saddened and scared him.

As they continued their journey through the valley, he found it hard to talk to Sarah or even to look her in the eye.

The two of them had been following behind Andrew and Galleon for several hours, but rather than talking to Sarah, Joshua found the silence more comforting.

"You're very quiet, Joshua," Sarah murmured.

"Oh, it's nothing, really," he said with a nervous chuckle. He avoided making eye contact with her, trying to pretend there was nothing wrong. It wasn't very convincing. For a moment, Joshua thought Sarah was going to say something else, but she just looked down with a sullen expression and they carried on walking in silence.

Galleon watched the graceful birds. He wondered what it would be like to fly through the sky, effortlessly carried by the thermals. It would be a much faster way of travelling throughout the land and perhaps this would bring him closer to knowing whether other Imps still existed.

Rays of brilliant sunshine pieced through gaps in the clouds to illuminate a small flock of Raetheons soaring above them. They glided gracefully and effortlessly through the valley. Swerving side to side, they rode the updrafts, barely moving their wings.

Sarah was commenting on how adorable and majestic the peaceful Raetheons were when a dark cloud appeared in the sky behind them. As it accelerated towards the Raetheons, it became clear it was not a cloud.

A sense of horror overcame him. "Blood-bats!" Galleon screamed. "Quick, take cover!"

The other three froze, their eyes fixed on the rapidly approaching swarm.

"NOW!" Galleon shouted, pointing to the approaching danger. "Quickly! HIDE!"

He dove behind a large boulder. Everyone scattered and found somewhere to hide. None of them knew what Blood-bats were or why they should be hiding, but they trusted Galleon enough to follow his lead.

The dark swarm consisted of dozens of foul-looking black, bat-like creatures. They had dark, round, hairy bodies, and their wings consisted of a thin layer of a leathery material, the bones of their wing arms silhouetted through their wings. About half the size of a Raetheon, they were much faster and extremely agile. Galleon knew they had huge fangs and curved, pointed talons. The shrieking sound they made was horrifying.

One Blood-bat separated from the swarm and swooped down at high speed towards the circling Raetheons. The flock of white birds shrieked and scattered in all directions.

One separated from the flock, and the Blood-bat chased it farther away from the rest. The Raetheon twisted and turned but the Blood-bat hounded it ruthlessly. Several more Blood-bats separated from the swarm and swooped down towards the lone Raetheon to join in the chase. It wasn't long before they reached it and all commenced savagely attacking their meal in mid-flight from all directions.

The slower and less agile Raetheon screeched as the Blood-bats all tore into its wings and torso until it began spiralling down to the earth. The Blood-bats continued their relentless attack on the poor Raetheon until it stopped moving altogether just before it struck the ground.

All the Blood-bats landed around it and tore ferociously at the lifeless carcass. Within minutes, it was stripped to the bone and the Blood-bats took off again down the valley. As they were disappearing, white Raetheon feathers were still falling to the ground.

When the Blood-bats were out of sight, Galleon emerged from behind the boulder that shielded him from view.

"It's OK. You can come out now," he whispered to the others, keeping his eye trained on the area of the sky where the flock of Blood-bats had departed.

"What were those creatures?" Andrew asked with a shaky voice as he stood up from behind a nearby bush. Joshua and Sarah also came out from their hiding place.

"That poor Raetheon," Sarah said. "They just tore the poor thing apart."

"Those things are Blood-bats," Galleon said. "Vicious creatures of the underworld. They are the Goat's eyes. He uses them to keep track of things."

"What were they doing here?" Joshua asked.

"I'm not sure," Galleon said, shaking his head. "The Goat must be on the lookout for something. We'd better be careful. Perhaps we should find cover for the night. Blood-bats can see great distances, even in the dark, and they could come back."

Andrew pointed to a hut nearby. A plume of smoke was rising from it, so it had clearly been burned like all the others. It seemed otherwise intact and would at least provide some cover from the spying eyes of the Blood-bats.

Andrew led them all towards the hut and they went inside. It was little more than a charred shell of a home, but the roof was covered in thick layers of moss. Sarah suggested the moist moss was the reason the roof had not burned down like most of the other huts they had seen. Andrew started collecting bits of wood to make a fire.

"No!" Galleon snapped. "We can't light a fire, it's too risky. We can't risk being seen by the Blood-bats if they come back this way."

The others looked at him. They knew this would mean a cold night, but nobody questioned his judgement.

"We should get some rest for the night. I'll stay up and keep watch. Andrew, you can relieve me in a few hours, OK?"

Andrew nodded in agreement. They all settled in and tried to get comfortable.

None of them spoke for the next hour. As the evening swarms of Dengle bugs came out, the soothing humming sent Joshua, Sarah and Andrew off to sleep. Galleon lingered by the door. He kept surveying the sky for Blood-bats, but they never came back - at least not as far as he could tell.

After the others had fallen into a deep sleep, he sat down and picked up Joshua's keeper bag. He pulled out one of the two cloth-wrapped orbs and unravelled it. It was the Orb of Vision Melachor had traded with them.

Galleon recalled Melachor had said something about this orb opening up a portal through which he escaped the onslaught of the Goat many years ago. How did it work? He sat there, studying the orb, contemplating whether it was just a crystal or whether it might help him find other Imps.

He tried to stay awake but fatigue from the journey took over and his body begged for rest. The intoxicating hum of Dengles was like a lullaby. It was so comforting, he felt himself becoming drowsy, until his head fell forwards and he drifted off to sleep.

As Galleon slept, the orb, still clutched in his hands, started glowing. A hideous image of the Goat appeared inside the orb. His dark eyes shifted around, locking onto Galleon's face.

The Goat's eyes narrow as He peered into Galleon's eyes. The Imp's subconscious thoughts began filling with the Goat's image. It was like a dream but it felt very real. Galleon felt weightless and floating in a dark space. He could hear whimpering off to one side but couldn't see who or what it was. The only thing he was aware of was the Goat's image: that evil and menacing face floating before him.

The two of them made eye contact.

"What do you want?" Galleon asked. His lips didn't move as he spoke. He tried to understand the telepathic link between them, but his thoughts turned to his loathing for the foul creature.

"You know who I am." The Goat's voice echoed inside Galleon's head.

"Yes," Galleon sneered. "You murdered my people."

The Goat said nothing. He narrowed His eyes and tilted His head forward. The whites beneath His eyes made Him look even more menacing.

"No," the Goat said after a few moments. "They are not dead, they are alive. All of them are still alive. I can return them to your realm."

Galleon pondered this. Was it a lie? Was the Goat trying to trick him in some way?

"It is neither a lie nor a trick," the Goat said.

"What do you want in return?"

"The boy who seeks the orbs. Give him to me and I will return your people to you unharmed. What is one life compared to so many?"

Galleon stared at the Goat in disbelief. He was being asked to betray Joshua, the man who rescued him from that trap, who was helping him search for other Imps.

"You owe this boy nothing. He cannot help you find what you seek."

Galleon realised the Goat was reading his thoughts. "And if I don't?"

"Then I will kill your people," the Goat replied with a hideous cackle, "all of them! And when I've killed the last of them, I will kill you too."

The Goat's image receded into the darkness.

"Galleon? Galleon! GALLEON!" Andrew shouted, pushing the slumbering Imp hard on the shoulder to wake him.

"Wake up!"

Galleon shook his head in confusion and peered around. Andrew was standing over him, gripping his shoulder.

"What? Oh…yes, right. Sorry."

"What's the matter with you? I thought you were supposed to be keeping watch! Anyway, it's my turn now so you may as well get comfortable."

Galleon quickly wrapped the orb in the cloth and returned it to Joshua's keeper bag.

"What were you doing with the orb?" Andrew whispered.

"Oh, um, nothing. I just wanted to take a closer look at it, that's all."

"It'll be dawn in a few hours," Andrew whispered. "You'd better get some rest. With those Blood-bat things flying around, we'll all need to be alert."

"Right," Galleon said, still dazed. "I'll, um, I'll just get settled down here, then. See you in the morning."

Galleon found a spot and curled up on the ground. He wondered whether the encounter with the Goat was just a dream. If it was real, was the Goat's offer a genuine one? Would Galleon be prepared to betray Joshua and the others in exchange for the return of his people?

With the pulsating humming of the Dengles and these thoughts tossing and turning in his mind, he drifted off to sleep.

CHAPTER SIXTEEN
Galleon's Temptation

The following morning Joshua, Sarah and Galleon woke to find Andrew standing guard at the door.

"Have you seen anything?" Galleon asked Andrew, yawning.

Galleon had slept awkwardly during the night and was now stretching to one side, holding his hip. He still had the Goat on his mind and wondered whether the others suspected anything.

"Nothing," Andrew replied, staring through the doorway and peering around, shaking his head. "A few Raetheons every now and then, but that's about it. I think the Blood-bats have moved on."

"Is everything all right, Galleon?" Sarah asked.

"Of course, I'm all right." He straightened and glared at Sarah. "Why wouldn't I be?"

She recoiled from him, her face crumpling.

"I'm sorry. I mean, of course I'm fine. We're all fine."

He let out a forced chuckle. All three of the others looked at him and then at each other.

"Well," Sarah suggested, "it's just that you look like you're in pain or something. I just wondered if you were OK, that's all."

"Oh," Galleon said with a nervous chuckle. "Right, yes, well, it's just a bit of cramp that's all. I've slept on coarse gravel that was more comfortable than this floor."

He ended with another nervous laugh and bounced on his feet a couple of times. He was worried about revealing anything about his vision with the Goat during the night. He needed time to think it over and didn't want to discuss it with the others.

"I think I might have some Yucust salve in my keeper bag," Sarah suggested. "Here, it'll make you feel much better."

"Oh, right," Galleon said, trying to act normally again. "Well, if you think it will help?"

Sarah rummaged around in her keeper bag and pulled out a small jar of the pale, gooey paste and handed it to Galleon.

"Here you go," she said with a smile.

Galleon looked at the jar, then at Sarah and then at the jar again. He unscrewed the lid and sniffed its contents. Dipping his finger into the jar, he pulled out a dollop of the paste, and was just about to put it into his mouth.

"NO!" Sarah cried, grabbing for Galleon's hand. "You just rub it on to where it hurts."

Everyone laughed and the mood in the hut lifted. They all packed their things together, set out into the sunlit valley and continued their journey.

"Is it helping?" Joshua asked Galleon, pointing to his hip.

"Actually, yes, it is. I feel much better. Quite an amazing young woman isn't she?"

Joshua smiled and nodded.

As they walked, Sarah was telling Andrew all about how to make Yucust salve and why it was so good at alleviating pain.

"It's a complicated procedure. First, you have to grind dried Yucust roots to a fine powder. Then you leave the powder to soak for several days in Bramock berry juice."

"How much berry juice do you add?"

Joshua felt sure Andrew wouldn't remember any of this but was glad his best friend was at least showing interest in what Sarah was saying. As long as they were busy talking to each other, he would have some time to himself to mull things over.

"About equal parts," Sarah went on. "It's important to remove all the husks first, though, otherwise you won't get the right consistency. Eventually, it will turn into a sticky paste. You heat this until it starts to turn pale yellow with a runny texture. Then you mix it thoroughly until the yellow colour completely disappears, leaving a transparent, gooey paste."

Andrew kept nodding as if he was taking it all in. Galleon in the meantime joined Joshua. Joshua sensed something was on Galleon's mind but wasn't sure what to do about it. He was mulling over various ways of how to tackle the subject when Galleon broke the silence.

"What would you place more value on, Joshua?" Galleon asked. "Your entire village or your best friend?"

"What do you mean?"

"Well, let's suppose you had to pick between losing everyone in your village or losing Andrew, or perhaps Sarah? Which would you choose?"

Joshua thought this an odd question but pondered it before answering.

"Well, I don't really know," he replied, being as truthful as he could.

"I've never really thought about it. I supposed I'd have to be in that situation before I knew what I'd do. Why do you ask?"

"Oh, nothing, nothing. Just trying to keep my mind occupied."

He wouldn't look Joshua in the eye. Instead, he just stared ahead as they walked, even though Joshua kept his eyes on him.

By around noon they decided to stop for a rest, finding shelter from the midday sun beneath an Ashfer. Joshua sat and rummaged in his keeper bag and took out the two orbs. He noticed Galleon watching him nervously. Joshua unwrapped them both and held the spherical crystals one in each hand.

"How do you suppose these things work?" he asked.

Galleon stared at the orbs and shook his head slowly as Joshua passed the Orb of Vision to him. It was the same orb the Imp had encountered last night. He reached out with some hesitation before taking it. He kept his gaze fixed on the spherical crystal as Joshua spoke to him.

"Didn't Melachor say something about using the orb to open up some sort of portal? What did he do to make that happen?"

Galleon was listening but not paying attention. As he stared into the orb, the sound of Joshua's voice faded until the only sound he could hear was his own breathing. He kept staring at the orb, and a murky image appeared.

Suddenly, Galleon felt himself floating in a dark room and once again staring at the Goat's face. He felt disconnected from his body just has he had done last night.

"Have you considered my offer, Imp?" said an ominously familiar, husky voice.

The image of the Goat floated in front of him but His lips weren't moving and the words seemed to come from inside Galleon's head.

"Why should I trust you? How do I know you'll uphold your end of the bargain?"

Galleon was unable to stifle his loathing for the foul creature, but at the same time he admitted the thought of being with his own kind again was tempting. A hideous smile crept across the Goat's face. It lasted briefly before turning into a growl.

"Tell me! Where is the boy?"

Galleon sensed the Goat was becoming frustrated.

"Why should I? What's the matter? Don't you trust your own Blood-bats to find us? What do you want with my friend anyway?"

Galleon sensed the Goat was somehow scared of Joshua but couldn't quite put his finger on it. The connection established through the Orb of Vision seemed to be allowing thoughts to pass both ways between them. He tried to read the Goat's mind, but it teemed with a jumble images and echoes. He struggled to understand it all. Each time he thought the disconnected images were starting to make sense, the imagery would change. Was the Goat trying to hide something? Was it the orbs? Why didn't the Goat want Joshua to find all the orbs?

Sensing the Imp was starting to read his thoughts, the Goat disciplined his mind and tried to distract his opponent.

"Wouldn't you like to see your own kind freed again? Or would you prefer to see them suffer?"

The Goat smiled again. Galleon started to hear what might be a distant scream. As it grew louder in his mind, it became clearer. It was the unmistakable voice of someone being tortured, and the frightening noise horrified him.

Galleon's mind filled with dread as the sound of Imps screaming in pain flooded his mind. He tried to push the thoughts aside but he was powerless to prevent it. The Goat had complete control over what he wanted Galleon to think.

The sound of his kin being tortured was sheer agony, and his mind filled with rage as his anguish reached unbearable levels. Galleon thought he could take it no more. He shut his eyes and tried to drown out the noise of the suffering, but the more he tried, the more intense it became until he felt overwhelmed. The tormented Imp was totally paralysed with fear.

"Galleon?" Joshua said, nudging him a couple of times. "GALLEON!" Still, he didn't move. Joshua looked at Sarah and Andrew.

"What's wrong with him?" Andrew asked.

"I don't know. I think it might have something to do with the orb he's holding," Joshua said.

"What are we going to do? We can't just leave him here like this."

"If I could just…" Joshua tried to remove the orb from Galleon's clenched hand but his grip was too tight.

"I can't get it loose. Quickly! Think of something!"

"Andrew! Do you still have that liquorice moss?" Sarah asked.

"Oh, yes! I forgot about that." Andrew reached into his keeper bag and pulled out some of the treat from Fable & Florelle's inn. He wafted it under Galleon's nose. As the Imp sniffed it, he slowly came around.

"What? Where? What's going on?"

Galleon snapped out of his trance and shook his head, dazed. Andrew slipped the liquorice moss back into his keeper bag.

"Are you all right?" Joshua asked. "You really don't seem yourself today. You sort of faded out there. You scared us."

"Um, sorry, you were saying?"

Joshua frowned and his gaze lingered.

"Come on Andrew, let's see if we can find something to eat," Sarah said. The two of them wandered off, leaving Joshua and Galleon behind.

"So, the orb? I was asking you how you think it works?"

"Um…well…I'm sure I don't know."

The pair of them chatted for much of the afternoon but Galleon was still trying to make sense of what happened with the orb. He was again unsure if he had simply dreamed the encounter with the Goat. They had been walking for a long time and the sun was intense, so maybe it was an illusion after all. It seemed so real to him but it also seemed as if no time had elapsed. He felt disoriented and didn't know whether he should trust his senses. Galleon contemplated telling Joshua what had happened, but then Sarah and Andrew returned with some food.

Sarah had been showing Andrew how to snare Flarrets. Andrew was reeling from his success of having caught his first Flarret using Sarah's much more successful technique. Galleon didn't say very much as they sat and cooked the pair of Flarrets over an open fire. He found he couldn't get the sound of the screaming out of his head but he was also wrestling with his loyalties. He wanted to be with his own kind and his family again.

Joshua also remained quiet. He was still avoiding Sarah, who tried several times to strike up a conversation with him. Each time she tried, he found an innocent excuse to get up and go and busy himself with something. After a while, Sarah gave up trying and just sat quiet instead.

As the Flarrets cooked over Andrew's campfire, everyone sat in sombre silence. As usual, Andrew was the last to pick up on the subtle clues around him.

"You must be looking forward to going back home again, Sarah?" he asked, turning to her as he removed the last bit of meat from his Flarret leg.

Sarah had been sitting in silence, looking at Joshua with a vacant stare. She turned to Andrew.

"Hmmm?" she said, and raising her brow. "Oh, yes, home. Yes, I'm looking forward to seeing everyone again. This journey has been really good, and I've learned lots of new things but, um, yes, I am looking forward to seeing home again." She managed a fake smile that was probably good enough to convince Andrew but not the others.

"Will you stay there when you get back?" Andrew asked. Joshua shifted on his seat at the question. Andrew had a tendency to say things without grasping their significance. Sarah looked back at Joshua. He cast her a fleeting glance, then feigned interest in the piece of Flarret he was eating.

"I...I don't know," she whispered.

She kept her gaze on Joshua.

"I'm not really sure what my future holds."

Joshua finished with his Flarret and looked around to try to find something to distract him. He reached into his keeper bag and took out the orbs.

"What are those markings?" Andrew asked, his voice muffled by a mouthful of Flarret.

Joshua took out the orbs and laid them on the ground.

"This is the one that the Oracle gave me," he said, showing Andrew the orb with the engraving of an hourglass.

"She said it was the Orb of Time."

"So what's the other one then?" Andrew motioned to the other orb. Joshua showed Andrew the engraving of an eye on the side of the other crystal.

"The Oracle called it the Orb of Vision," Joshua said, studying the orb in more detail.

Galleon was staring expectantly. As Joshua peered into the orb and his eyes started glazing over.

Galleon sat up straight and shouted, "STOP!"

He reached for the orb and snatched it from Joshua's hand. He wrapped it back in its cloth and tucked it into Joshua's keeper bag. The others looked at him with puzzled faces.

"What's the matter?" Joshua asked.

"Look," Galleon said, letting out a big sigh. "I should have told you this earlier, but I wasn't sure if it was real or not."

"Told us what?" Joshua asked.

"I had an encounter with the orb last night and again just now before we started eating. I saw the Goat. He used the orb to talk to me. I wanted to tell you before but I wasn't sure if I had dreamed it or not."

"What did the Goat want?" Joshua asked. Everyone sat up and leaned in.

Galleon paused before answering and let out another sigh.

"It's you, Joshua. He wants you," Galleon said, as he looked at the ground with his lower lip quivering.

"He knows you have the Orb of Vision and he knows you were looking for the Oracle. He's desperate to prevent you from finding all three orbs."

Joshua stood up and walked around trying to piece it all together.

"How would He know I was looking for the Oracle?"

"Melachor." Andrew snorted. "He's the only other person that knows. He must be working for the Goat."

Joshua shook his head.

"Maybe. Or he could have been captured by the Goat. So the Goat doesn't know we have the Orb of Time yet?"

"I don't think so. He's desperately afraid of you finding all three orbs. I could sense the thought of it terrified Him."

Joshua tried to remember what the Oracle had told him. It was all starting to make sense. The Oracle had said the one that had banished her children was also seeking the power of the orbs. But why? What was it about opening up the Portallas that scared the Goat so much?

"We need to get moving." Joshua proclaimed. "If He's looking for the orbs, there's no time to delay. We have to get to Jemarrah and find the third orb there before He does."

Everyone stood up and collected their things. Andrew stamped out the fire, and the four of them set off north through the valley.

CHAPTER SEVENTEEN

Enduring Love

The travellers reached the northernmost end of the Valley of Moross by the following day. They climbed over the final foothills where the twin mountain ranges gave way to a more familiar landscape of forests and woodland.

The sight of trees undulating into the distance stretched to the horizon. Their vantage point was high enough to give them a view of distant flocks of Raetheons flying beneath them across the treetop canopy. Joshua felt a sense of relief at leaving the rocky mountains. No more caves or patches of dry and barren land.

They would all be much safer under the cover of the forest canopy, out of sight from the prying eyes of Blood-bats. He knew the Goat was looking for him, and he still worried he was putting the others in great danger, but there was something comforting about the forest terrain sprawling out before him.

For a brief moment, he forgot about the Goat, Blood-bats and the pressures he was under. Closing his eyes, he spread his arms and allowed the breeze to rush over him.

Joshua's tensions continued to ease as they made their way down and into the forest. He even found himself relaxing to the point he wanted to get closer to Sarah again.

"I bet you're really looking forward to seeing your village again," he said to Sarah as they rested under the shade of an Ashfer. Andrew and Galleon had gone off in search of some Flame-bark.

Joshua was feeling guilty about his recent behaviour towards Sarah. Keeping his distance from her, as he had done over the past couple of days, weighed heavily on his mind. It was clear she was upset, and he felt a deep remorse at having been responsible for that.

Sarah looked at him but didn't answer him straight away.

"Have I done something to upset you, Joshua?"

Sarah's voice trembled and there was a quiver in her lower lip. Joshua sensed she was close to tears and this saddened him further.

"No...no, of course not." Joshua put a comforting hand on her shoulder.

"Well, you've hardly said two words to me since we left the cave."

Joshua could see she was almost in tears.

"I don't understand what I've done to upset you."

She lowered her head and started sobbing. Joshua's heart sank, as the realisation hit him just how upset she had been these past days. Unable to hold back his own tears, he sat beside her and tenderly put his arm around her.

She turned to look at him. Seeing a tear roll down his face, she threw her arms around him in a tight embrace. Joshua held her and the two of them sat there and hugged with their heads on each other's shoulders, crying and comforting each other.

Joshua thought about what the Oracle had said but he decided enough was enough and he would hold back no longer. The pain it was causing was too much for him to bear. Whatever reason the Oracle had for telling him his love for Sarah could not last, it was too high a price to pay.

After a while, Joshua and Sarah released each other. Joshua very tenderly put both hands on either side of Sarah's face. Her skin was soft and warm. Using his thumb, he gently wiped a tear from her cheek. Her smile melted his heart. He gazed into her innocent eyes and felt a warm sensation in his stomach. Slowly and tenderly, he pulled her towards him. They tilted their heads, closed their eyes, and their lips touched.

The kiss was gentle and loving. Joshua's whole being was filled with a warm and contented feeling. It was like nothing he had ever experienced. Their kiss lingered. Joshua could feel the tears still rolling down Sarah's cheek.

After their kiss, Sarah and Joshua both looked at each other and each wiped a tear from the other's cheek at the same time. This made them both laugh, and they hugged each other again.

Joshua closed his eyes and enjoyed the warm embrace. He felt such relief at being able to show Sarah his true feelings, and he didn't want it to end. For that brief second in time when they kissed, nothing else mattered, and he lost himself in the moment. There was no Goat, no journey, no orbs or Oracles, nothing but his unwavering love for Sarah. It was pure bliss.

"What was it, Joshua? What did the Oracle say to cause you such pain?"

He heaved a big sigh and his shoulders sank. Sarah took his hand and held it tightly with both of hers. There was a long pause before he spoke.

"I only have a few memories of my father," he murmured, shaking his head slowly, looking at the ground. "But they are happy memories. I loved him dearly. More than anything, I want him to be proud of me: who I have become. It would make Mum so happy if we could be a family again."

He turned to Sarah and looked her in the eye.

"It's hard to lose someone you love. The Oracle told me I would have to give up my love for you."

He shook his head and his lip quivered.

"It isn't fair. I don't want to go through that pain again."

Sarah threw her arms around him and they embraced.

"Whatever happens, we'll face it together."

As they sat there holding each other, Galleon and Andrew were making their way back. When the two of them got closer, Galleon noticed Joshua and Sarah sitting together in an embrace and stopped in his tracks. He turned to Andrew, who was walking a few paces behind him.

"Um, d'you know what, Andrew? The clouds are clearing and it looks like it'll be cold tonight. I don't think we have enough Flame-bark. Come on, let's go find some more."

Andrew, who hadn't yet seen Joshua and Sarah, looked at Galleon with a puzzled expression, but followed him back into the woods anyway.

Joshua and Sarah eventually released each other. Joshua laughed and Sarah giggled. Now that she was starting to make those infectious giggles once more, Joshua felt that warm sensation inside all over again.

"Come on," Joshua couldn't stop beaming. "We'd better clear the ground for the fire before the others get back."

"I hope Andrew's aim has improved," he said, as he began clearing the leaf-litter from the floor. "I'm so hungry, I could eat a Raetheon."

Sarah glared at him.

"What? You wouldn't dare! How could you? I mean, you would never kill a poor, defenceless Raetheon, would you?"

She was staring at him with her brow lowered and both hands on her hips.

Joshua laughed again.

"Of course I wouldn't."

Sarah scowled at him with a grin for thinking such a horrible thing.

"I'd never eat anything as majestic as a Raetheon," he added.

Sarah smiled. She was happy to see Joshua was able to laugh and be funny again.

"Besides," he went on with a smile creeping across his face, "I never did like the taste of the damn things."

"Oh, you beast," Sarah laughed and threw some twigs at him. Joshua ducked. The pair laughed as they carried on clearing the forest floor.

Galleon and Andrew emerged into the small glade from the forest. Each of them was weighed down with a load of Flame-bark. Thanks to Galleon, they had brought more than enough to warm them through the night. As an added bonus, Andrew had a pair of Chirvels hanging across his shoulder.

"I see your aim has improved," Joshua said with a smile.

Andrew and Galleon threw the Flame-bark onto the ground. "I see your mood has improved," he retorted with a wink.

Joshua and Sarah looked at each other and smiled.

Andrew got the fire going and Sarah prepared the two Chirvels. Between Andrew's game and all the Flame-bark, the four of them ate well and enjoyed a warm night around the fire.

Sarah spent much of the evening telling the others all about her village and her life as she grew up in Jemarrah. Joshua was glad to see her bubbly enthusiasm was back. He spent much of his time just listening to the sound of her voice and peering into her eyes, grinning. He hadn't felt this relaxed and content for a long time and was enjoying just being there in her presence.

As the Dengles and other small insects came alive, the four friends felt drowsy. Everyone found a spot around the fire to settle in for the night. Andrew was soon off to sleep, having eaten the most as usual. Sarah and Joshua sat by the fire holding hands until Sarah nodded off with her head falling onto his shoulder.

Galleon got up and stretched. He paced around the fire for a few minutes before Joshua's curiosity got the better of him.

"What's bothering you?"

Galleon continued pacing. He stared down and shook his head.

"I'm sorry, Joshua."

"What are you sorry about?"

Galleon hesitated. He took a deep breath and let out a sigh.

"I was tempted. By the Goat, I mean, during my encounters with the Orb of Vision. He offered me a deal. He said he would return my people if I betrayed you. And...well...for a brief moment, I considered His offer."

Joshua thought for a few moments before looking up at Galleon.

"It must have been a very difficult decision for you. I can see why you were tempted. I'm glad you didn't, though. I think you chose to do the right thing, Galleon. After all, there's no reason to trust He'd keep His word. It's our actions that define us, my friend. Don't worry about it. I think I know how you feel."

Joshua thought about how he would feel if his and Galleon's positions were reversed, and it was Sarah or perhaps Andrew that the enemy had captured.

"What did the Goat say when you refused?"

Galleon snorted. "He threatened to kill me and my family."

"Certainly sounds like someone not to be trusted to me. Maybe He would have done that even if you did give Him what He wants."

Galleon raised his brow and nodded.

"That's a good point."

Galleon stopped pacing and looked for a comfortable place by the fire. He curled up on the ground and settled down for the night. With a final yawn, he closed his eyes and drifted off to sleep.

Joshua gently put his arm around Sarah with his cheek resting against her head. The soothing hum of Dengles hung in the air as the fire crackled through the night. It wasn't long before he, too, fell asleep.

Christopher D. Morgan

CHAPTER EIGHTEEN
Orb of Time

As the early mist lifted, Joshua awoke and found himself resting against a log in front of the smouldering remains of the fire. Sarah's head lay against his chest, cradled in his arm. She was fast asleep. He looked down at her face and smiled. Lifting his hand, he caressed the side of her cheek. A smile spread across her face and she gave a deep sigh.

Joshua reached for his keeper bag, carefully removed one of the orbs and unwrapped the cloth from around it. It was the Orb of Time and he studied the hourglass shape carved into one side of it. As he looked closer, the clear crystal clouded up on the inside. There was a swirling motion, like a hurricane was forming inside the orb.

There was a blinding flash and Joshua felt disconnected from his body and floating in the air. He could hear what he thought to be a woman crying but the scene coming into focus before him was hazy and indistinct.

The disembodied Joshua looked around the room for a clue as to where he was but he couldn't move or feel his body. The image around him cleared, and he got a better sense of things.

He was inside a Woodsman's hut, and there was a fireplace burning over to one side. There was screaming and noises of pandemonium, like a battle was taking place. It sounded like it was coming from right outside the hut.

A Warrior burst through the front door and dashed across to the bed on the far side of the room. A woman was lying there. She cradled a newborn, and there was another woman wiping the child clean. There was blood on the sheets from where she had just given birth. The tunic colours of the Warrior and woman were from his own tribe.

"Please don't let them take our baby!" the woman cried.

"Don't worry. I'll protect you," the Warrior reassured her.

He wiped her brow with a wet cloth from a bowl beside the bed.

"Joshua? Joshua!" the man called out.

A child came running into the hut from another room, and the man picked him up. The small boy looked to be about three years old.

"I'll take our son somewhere safe. Don't worry, I'll be back for you soon."

"No! Don't, don't leave me, please," the woman pleaded.

"Don't worry. I'll be back as soon as I can. I have to get Joshua to safety first."

The man left with the boy in his arms and the woman carried on sobbing. The midwife scurried around in panic.

The Warrior came back through the door but the boy was no longer with him. Another Warrior followed him but he belonged to another tribe. Joshua didn't recognise the green and red tunic of the second Warrior.

The two men fought fiercely with each other. They struggled and knocked the midwife to the floor, screaming, as they jostled about the small hut. They both had knives drawn and each was trying to reach the other's throat.

As the struggle ensued, they fell onto the bed and landed on the woman, who let out an almighty shriek of pain. Another Morelle Warrior came running through the door. He grabbed the intruder and lifted him from the bed.

The two Morelle Warriors fought with the outsider and eventually managed to drag him out of the hut. Joshua looked back at the woman on the bed. She was holding the baby in her arms but it wasn't moving or making any sound. She held the newborn tight to her chest and was crying inconsolably.

"My baby," the grief-stricken woman cried, "my sweet, little girl."

Joshua looked on with amazement and horror. The newborn little girl was lifeless.

The woman's husband came running back into the hut. He had bloodstained hands and went over to the side of the bed and got down on one knee. He looked at the little girl and then at the crying woman. Tears ran down his cheeks.

"Our baby," the woman cried, "they killed our little girl."

She held the baby close to her chest and rocked back and forth on the bed. The horrified woman's heartbreaking tears tore at Joshua's heart.

The Warrior lowered his head, then looked up and let out bloodcurdling roar of grief.

"They will pay for this. I swear they will pay."

He was weeping and holding the woman's head to his shoulder. As Joshua looked on, the scene before him started fading.

He felt something pushing at him.

"Joshua? Joshua, snap out of it!"

Sarah was kneeling in front of him shaking his shoulders.

"Are you OK?" she asked.

"What? Where am I?" Joshua asked, moving his head side to side and slowly coming back to his senses.

"You're OK, you're safe. You just sort of froze for a while with that orb in your hand. I couldn't wake you. It scared me."

Andrew and Galleon were both standing behind Sarah and looking down at him.

"Are you OK?" Andrew asked.

"What happened?" Galleon asked. "What did you see?"

Joshua got up and looked at them each in turn. "I'm not really sure. I think I just saw my mother giving birth."

"I didn't know your mother was pregnant." Andrew asked.

"No, you don't understand. It was a long time ago. I think it was my sister she was giving birth to."

"I didn't know you had a sister." Andrew said, still looking puzzled.

"I don't," Joshua said shaking his head. "I mean I didn't think I had a sister either. It looked like she died in childbirth. There was a battle going on. I don't think he intended to kill her. It just sort of happened. There was this Warrior from another tribe that was fighting my dad. It happened just after my mother gave birth but the baby didn't survive."

Sarah held her hand to her mouth with a look of horror. "That's awful," she said, almost in tears.

156

"Are you sure it was your parents?" Galleon asked.

"I think so. It looked as though I was about three years old at the time."

He shook his head as he tried to remember back to his childhood.

"I don't remember this happening or my mother even being pregnant. Mum and Dad never said anything to me about having a sister who died at birth."

"What does it mean?" Sarah asked.

Joshua stared straight ahead and continued to shake his head.

"I don't know," he whispered.

It was an intense experience, and he was still processing it in his own mind. He started walking but wobbled on his feet. Andrew caught him and guided him to a nearby tree stump.

"Here," he said, helping him sit, "best you rest and collect your thoughts first."

Sarah sat next to him and held his hand with both of hers.

"I'm so sorry, Joshua, about your sister, I mean. It must have been terrible for you to witness that when you were young."

"That's OK," Joshua murmured. "I don't remember any of it, anyway. And besides, my dad took me away somewhere when it happened."

He looked down at the ground and heaved a big sigh.

"I just wish they had told me I had a sister."

Sarah caressed his hand.

"Well, maybe they thought you were too young and didn't want to burden you with it all?"

She squeezed his hand tightly. Joshua inhaled and forced a smile.

"Yes," he said turning to her, "maybe you're right."

"Did you recognise who the attacking tribe was?" Sarah asked.

"No, I didn't recognise the colours. It could have been from any tribe in Forestium," he said, trying hard to remember the details.

"There were certainly a lot more tribal wars back in those days."

Joshua picked up the orb again and looked at it. Sarah was talking to him and comforting him. He heard her voice fade away and saw the same swirling cloud forming inside the orb again.

There was another flash and Joshua found himself once again floating in mid-air, disconnected from reality. He was once more viewing a situation that took place long ago.

There was another tribal Warrior. Joshua didn't recognise the man but he did recognise the same green and red tunic from the earlier encounter with the orb. Whoever this was, he was from that same tribe that had attacked Morelle all those years ago when Joshua was a young child.

The man had deep blue eyes and blond hair. Joshua thought his face seemed familiar but he couldn't quite put his finger on it. As the scene cleared, Joshua could see more detail. He squinted to try to make out the features in the man's face.

He was there with a young woman and a little girl. They were playing and laughing together. It looked like a young family. As they played, another man with the same colours came bursting into the room.

"Marauders! In the village! Screechers report maybe a dozen men or more," the second man cried.

The first man stood up and spoke to the young woman.

"Here, take Sarah and hide! Quickly!"

The two men left the room. The woman picked up the little girl, cradled her head and left.

Joshua's mind was racing. Were these Sarah's parents he was seeing? He could hear the thumping of his own heartbeat. It echoed in his mind.

There was another flash and this time he was outside and the man he had just seen was fighting fiercely. He had a striking resemblance to Sarah, so he presumed it to be her father.

The man was fighting with one of the marauding Warriors. Joshua looked on with horror as he realised the marauders were wearing colours from his own Morelle tribe.

Sarah's father and the Morelle Warrior continued fighting fiercely with pandemonium going on all around them. Joshua tried to get a look at who the Morelle Warrior was but he could only see him from behind.

"Take Sarah and get out of here!" the fighting Warrior screamed.

Joshua could see Sarah's mother still cradling her and staring around in confusion. She had panic written all over her face as she tried to find a path out of harm's way.

As she scurried between the fighters, the man duelling with Sarah's father lunged with his knife. Sarah's father sidestepped the knife, but it continued straight into Sarah's mother as she tried to pass. She dropped the crying child to the ground and fell to her knees, clutching at her abdomen. She contorted in pain and keeled over with the baby, screaming.

"NO!" Sarah's father howled.

The man who had accidentally stabbed Sarah's mother froze, as did all the other fighters around him. He looked shocked at his own action. He threw his knife onto the ground, turned and ran.

As he turned, Joshua got a good look at the fleeing man's face. To his sheer horror, he saw it was his own father.

The scene faded. The echoes of screaming subsided, and the vision became indistinct.

"Joshua? JOSHUA!" Sarah shouted. "Wake up!"

Joshua opened his eyes and looked around in confusion. Tears were streaming down his face.

"It was him! I saw it. It was my father! He's the one. He's the one who did it."

He was breathing so heavily his head spun. Looking around frantically, he locked his eyes on Sarah.

She gazed at him with deep concern. "Joshua, calm down! Take slow, deep breaths!"

Joshua looked into her eyes, shook his head and started crying.

"I'm sorry," he said with tears streaming down his face. "It was an accident. He didn't mean to do it." Joshua was utterly distraught. He began to shake his head and cry inconsolably.

"He didn't mean to do it," he cried over and over. "He didn't mean to kill her. It was an accident."

Sarah threw her arms around him and held him tightly.

"Shhhhh," she reassured him. "It's OK. It'll all be OK, Joshua. I'm here. You're safe now."

Joshua held onto Sarah and continued to cry as the scenes he just witnessed swirled around in his head.

Andrew and Galleon looked on, unable to help. Galleon picked up the orb that was sitting on the ground. He wrapped it in the cloth and put it away into Joshua's keeper bag.

It took several minutes before Joshua calmed down to the point he could talk sense again. When he was ready he let go of

Sarah, who was still comforting him. He wiped his eyes and took several deep breaths.

"I think he wanted vengeance for the death of my sister," Joshua said after several minutes of sitting there in silent thought. "They raided your village, a dozen or so Morelle Warriors."

Sarah held onto his hand.

"You were just a baby."

Joshua's eyes filled with tears and his voice began to shake.

"Your mother was carrying you and trying to find a way out of the battle."

Joshua took a few more deep breaths. Everyone waited for him to describe the vision further. He found comfort gazing into Sarah's eyes.

Sarah looked concerned but she said nothing and allowed Joshua to take his time. All the while, she clung to his hand.

"Your father and mine were fighting," Joshua went on, "he...he..."

Joshua found it difficult to get the words out, "he didn't mean to stab her. I could see my father didn't mean it. She just dropped right there onto the ground. You fell. You were crying."

Tears formed and rolled down both Joshua's and Sarah's cheeks.

Joshua tried to make sense of how he had a sister that died at birth and that Sarah's mother had been killed at the hands of his father. Through some ironic twist of fate, the two of them had been brought together and now they had fallen love. Was this fate's way of reconciling the past? Was it a way to make amends for past deeds? All Joshua knew was that he was here at this moment, in this place and in love with this beautiful young woman.

Joshua and Sarah, both crying again, embraced each other and held on tightly. Andrew and Galleon looked at each other with disbelief. They, too, were welling up but were trying not to show it.

"We, um," Galleon hesitated, "we should…make a move. We'll, um, yes, we'll start packing up, I think."

He looked at Andrew and nodded. Andrew nodded back and the two of them started clearing everything away and stamping out the fire. Joshua and Sarah stood up after a few minutes. They continued to hold hands as they walked off into the forest.

Not long after they left the clearing, a Blood-bat, hanging upside down in the treetop above where they sat, unfurled its wings.

The Goat was pacing up and down in His dark room, furious. He snorted and His hooves clicked as He strode back and forth. As He leaned forward, His menacing eyes pierced through His fierce eyebrows. He shook His head violently and let out an ear-splitting roar. Melachor whimpered in the corner. He trembled as the Goat roared with rage.

"The boy has the Orb of Time," the Goat mumbled to himself. "He must not find the Orb of Suffering."

He stopped and looked at Melachor. The cowering man turned his head and held one hand to his face. He was petrified the Goat was going to torture him further.

"YOU!" the Goat roared, striding over to where Melachor was quivering on the floor. He stood over His petrified captive and stared down at the frail figure. With a swift flick of his foot,

He kicked Melachor in the side of the head. This sent the tortured soul rolling across the floor. When he landed, blood was oozing down the side of his head.

"Please don't kill me," Melachor pleaded, raising both hands to protect his bloodstained face. He was shaking and his voice was trembling.

"You will stop the boy from finding the Orb of Suffering!"

Melachor peered through his fingers to look at the Goat. He could barely see Him through his trembling hands and the blood dripping over his eyes.

"M-m-me?" he whimpered.

"I will send you back to stop the boy. Fail me, worthless wretch, and I will kill your family." His tone was malevolent.

"And when I'm done with them, I will kill you, slowly."

He peered at Melachor and a hideous grin spread across the Goat's face. The Goat's dark eyes were terrifying. Melachor had no doubt the vicious creature was able and willing to make good on His threat. He nodded meekly, as if to accept this task, albeit against his will. The Goat sneered. His influence over the tortured Melachor was absolute.

He picked up the Mirror of Prophecy and thrust it at Melachor's face. Melachor squinted at it through his fingers. As he watched, his own battered reflection gave way to a swirling image. The frightened man recoiled. The swirling cleared to reveal his hut in the forest. As he peered deeper into the mirror, the image sharpened and Melachor's eyes widened.

Suddenly, he found himself on the floor. He closed his eyes and shielded his face, still shaking with fear. He curled into a ball, terrified at what might happen next.

As he slowly opened his eyes, he found he was once again back in his own hut in the middle of the forest. Wherever the mirror had taken him, he was now back in a familiar place.

On the floor beside him was the Mirror of Prophecy. Still gripped with fear, he looked at it and wondered. Had it all been a dream? He felt his face. It still ached from where the Goat had kicked him. It couldn't have been a dream if he still felt the pain, he thought. This realisation terrified him further. Nervously, he reached for the mirror and cautiously turned it to face him. There, staring back at him was the image of the Goat.

"Remember, sniffling scum," the Goat's voice sounded through the mirror, "fail me and your family will die, slowly."

With that, the Goat's outline faded, leaving his own bloodstained image reflecting back at him. Still shaking with fear, he got to his feet. He knew what he had to do. Thinking of his wife and children, he collected his things and left the hut.

CHAPTER NINETEEN
The Metamorph

Joshua and the others continued to travel northwest towards Jemarrah. They had quickened their pace since learning the Goat was also seeking the orbs.

They hadn't come across any villages or settlements yet and decided it would be best to continue avoiding others as much as possible. They were on the lookout at all times.

Joshua was still shaken by his experience with the Orb of Time. He kept wondering why the orb had chosen to take him back to see those particular events in history. What purpose did it serve?

Andrew and Sarah had not had much luck catching Chirvels or any other forest animals for the past couple of days. This annoyed Andrew in particular, as he complained he was growing tired of boiled Shrooms again. When they stumbled into a Yucust in the middle of a glade, Andrew was the first to notice a swarm of Yucust-bees humming around half way up the tree.

"Hey, Yucust honey!"

"Where?" Sarah asked.

Andrew pointed to the third horizontal branch about half way up the tree. The hive was nestled between the branch and the main trunk.

"Hmmm," Sarah said peering up at the nest, "doesn't look like a big crop yet. I'd say the nest is still less than a year old."

"There could be more inside that we can't see. What I wouldn't give for a fist-full of Yucust honey right now," he said, licking his lips.

"You're not going to be able to dislodge any of the capsules with your slingshot," Sarah said shaking her head and staring at the nest. "They look like they're stuck to the top of the branch."

"Looks like an easy enough climb. There's plenty of vines. Shouldn't be too difficult. Anyway, I do this all the time back in Morelle."

"Are you sure that's wise, my friend?" Galleon said, looking up at the imposing tree. The third branch where the Yucust bee nest was lodged did look extremely high up.

Galleon shook his head and said, "It's a pretty long way to fall, Andrew. I know Yucust honey is tasty and all but, really, it's not worth the risk just to avoid another one of Sarah's boiled Shroom specials."

Andrew chuckled. He removed his keeper bag and belt and laid them on the ground. He walked around the tree trying to assess the best way to get up to the nest.

Joshua, Sarah and Galleon stepped back and found a spot that gave them the best vantage from which to watch his progress.

Andrew pulled on two or three of the vines in turn. He grabbed the one that clung most securely to the trunk of the tree and started climbing.

He made swift progress all the way up to the first horizontal branch before the vine he clung to started to thin out and lose its grip on the tree trunk. Reaching over, he grabbed onto a thicker vine, manoeuvred his body around the trunk and was able to continue his ascent from there.

Andrew was a good climber and seemed to know which vines would safely take his weight. As he neared the second horizontal branch, he again reached over towards a thicker vine.

Just as he did this, his foot slipped. He was holding on to the thinning vine securely with both hands, but his feet were thrashing about trying to find a foothold.

Joshua, Sarah and Galleon sprang to their feet and watched helplessly as Andrew struggled to find his footing. Sarah gasped and put her hand to her mouth. There was a creaking sound as the vine he was clinging to tore away from the main trunk. It continued to loosen its grip on the tree until it broke free with a snap, and Andrew came crashing down to the ground.

His leg hit a protruding root and folded beneath him as he landed. Andrew let out an almighty scream as he grasped at his lower leg, and Joshua feared the worst. Everyone rushed over and knelt beside him. Sarah carefully felt his leg in several places.

"It's broken," she declared with a sigh and a shake of her head.

Andrew continued to scream in agony.

"We need a splint, something to hold the bones together."

They all looked around to see what was available. As they did so, a Raetheon came gliding across the glade and swooped in towards the travellers. It got closer and closer and just when it was a few paces away it flapped its huge, white wings a few times, hovered just above the ground and gently landed.

It folded its wings and stood there proudly. At full height, it was easily as tall as Joshua, and it just stood there, peering into Joshua's eyes.

Raetheons were normally very skittish creatures and so everyone was surprised at how close to them this one landed. The distraction was enough for Andrew to stop screaming for a moment, but then he turned his attention back to his misshapen leg and started groaning.

The Raetheon walked in closer and then, to everyone's astonishment, morphed into the figure of a Woodsman.

Joshua, Sarah and Galleon all backed a few steps away. The man looked at them but said nothing and walked over to where Andrew was still clutching at his lower leg.

He knelt beside Andrew and placed one of his hands on the broken leg. Andrew recoiled and looked at the others. They were just as baffled, wondering what it was this strange person or thing was going to do.

The man studied Andrew's leg for a moment and then looked at him. "I'm sorry, Andrew, but this is going to hurt."

He spoke in a calm tone.

"Brace yourself!"

Without further warning, he pulled on Andrew's leg. Andrew let out an agonised shriek. The man then held his hand over Andrew's now straightened leg and began waving it slowly from side to side. Andrew's leg began glowing green as the man moved his hand back and forth.

Andrew's screaming lessened with each wave of the man's hand. Within a matter of seconds Andrew stopped complaining altogether, and the green glow faded. He just stared at the others with his jaw dropped. "The...the pain...it's gone."

He stood up, looked down at his now healed leg and then at the man. "Thanks."

A grin formed across his face. "Um, who are you?"

"A friend," the man said with a smile. He turned to Joshua.

"I'm Protello. I've been following you since you left the cave."

Everyone looked at each other with puzzled faces.

"Why have you been following us?" Joshua asked. He had lots of questions but this was his immediate concern. The man didn't answer right away. He instead scanned the glade.

Suddenly, he fixed is eyes on something in the distance. Everyone else followed his gaze but couldn't see anything unusual. The man took a slingshot from his belt and launched a projectile across the glade at a blistering speed. It flew through a screen of leaves and struck something just out of sight.

A huge Blood-bat fell to the ground and remained motionless. Everyone looked at each other again with widened eyes.

"You should all get out of sight; you're not as safe here as you think you are, not even in the forest. Come, friends, He has eyes everywhere and you should stay out of the open before the rest of his Blood-bats spot you."

Protello led them out of the glade and back into the wood. When they were safely under the cover of the forest canopy, he turned around.

"Um, how did you know there was a Blood-bat hiding in the trees?" Joshua asked, trying to be as polite as he could.

"Forget that!" Andrew shouted. "How did you learn how to grow wings and then hide them again?"

The stranger held his arm out with his palm face-up. A Raetheon tail feather slowly appeared there out of thin air. It was white at first but quickly turned green. The man handed it to Joshua.

"He's a Metamorph," Galleon said. Joshua, Sarah and Andrew all turned to Galleon.

"That's right, my little friend," Protello said, looking down at him. "You've heard of us?"

"I've heard tales of Metamorphs. Until just now, that's all I ever thought they were, tales. It's said that a green tail feather of a Raetheon is the sign of a Metamorph."

Protello smiled.

"Um, a Metamorph?" Andrew asked. "What exactly is a Metamorph?"

"We have magical powers. I can become other creatures," Protello said, turning to Andrew. "From the smallest of bugs to a majestic bird, or," he said, using both hands to gesture to himself as he bowed, "even a humble Woodsman."

"And apparently you also have the power to heal?" Sarah said. The man looked at her and smiled.

"Each of us is special in our own way. My abilities are just different to yours, that's all. I've been most impressed with your skills, Sarah."

She smiled and blushed.

"You said you had been following us since the cave." Joshua asked. "Why?"

"The Oracle sent us to watch over you."

"Us?" Joshua asked, looking around. "You mean there are others like you?"

"There aren't many of my kind left. We have suffered at the hands of the Goat, just like the Imps and the people of the valley, as well as others that have displeased Him."

"Do you know what happened to them all...the Imps and the others?" Galleon asked.

"They are still alive, my friend. They are held captive in another realm."

"What makes you certain of that?"

"The Goat would not kill them. That would deny Him the pleasure of tormenting them further."

"What's this other realm?" Joshua asked.

"The world you know, this world you call Forestium, is but one of many worlds. They are bound together by the Portallas."

Joshua thought for a moment. The Oracle had said something about finding his father on the other side once he opened the Portallas.

"The Goat has the power to banish people from this world. But only when the Portallas has been opened can you move freely between the worlds."

"So all my people are still alive and in another world?" Galleon asked.

"Your people and many more besides, yes. They lack the power to return to this world."

He turned to Joshua.

"You must find the third orb, Joshua. Bring all three orbs together and open the Portallas. Only then can you free your father and the others that are held captive on the other side."

Joshua considered the man.

"But why me? Can't anyone open this Portallas thing?"

"Your path was chosen long ago, Joshua. You must trust your destiny. Open the Portallas and free those taken from this world! I must leave you now."

"Wait!" Joshua pleaded. "There's so much more I still need to know."

"There is no time. The Goat will stop at nothing to prevent you from finding the orbs. We will need all our cunning if we are to protect you, Joshua, but you must open the Portallas."

He took a couple of steps backward and morphed back into a Raetheon. Flexing his majestic white wings, he flew up to the treetop canopy and disappeared.

CHAPTER TWENTY
The Trader's Post

Joshua and the others stood there, bemused by what they had just seen. Other than Galleon, none of them had ever heard of Metamorphs before, much less seen one in the flesh.

Joshua's mind was racing. He was starting to put all the pieces together. Now, more than ever, he knew what he had to do. He had to find the third orb, bring all three together and open the Portallas to free everyone on the other side, including his father. With the lives of so many others resting on this plan, the burden of responsibility weighed on his mind.

As the four of them continued their journey towards the northern tip of Forestium, they came upon a village. It was the first village Joshua and Andrew had seen since leaving the Valley of Moross. Perhaps a little bigger than Joshua's home village, it was a bustling place. Most of the activity was centred around a cluster of buildings, accessed by several well-trodden paths. Huge forest Shires pulled carts up and down. A man on one of them was yelling at a couple of children, who were darting about between the carts and spooking the Shires.

Several Traders were engaged in an animated discussion over a roll of cloth one of them was showing the others.

"These colours look familiar," Sarah said as she noticed the Woodsman tunics. "I think I've seen Traders with them in Jemarrah before."

"We must be close to Jemarrah, then?" Joshua suggested.

"I'm not sure. Traders travel all over. I've never been to this village before so I don't know. Maybe we should ask someone?"

"Maybe we should find somewhere to eat first?" Andrew suggested. "I'm starving."

Galleon nodded.

"There must be an inn or something in the village somewhere," Joshua suggested. "Let's see if we can find one."

The four of them headed towards the main cluster of buildings. The squealing of a Chirvel caught Joshua's attention. It was standing on the edge of the roof of one of the larger buildings set back from the main footpath. Beneath its eaves where the Chirvel was standing on its hind legs was a door with a placard fixed to it. It read 'The Trader's Post'. There were several wooden tables and chairs outside with people sitting there drinking from brown mugs.

"Let's try here," Joshua suggested, and he led his friends to take a look.

Inside, it was similar in size to Fable & Florelle's but it was much cleaner and brighter. There was a central counter, surrounded by wooden tables with chairs. All the tables had clean, white tablecloths on them and the floor was neatly swept.

About half a dozen Traders were dotted around the place. Sunlight streamed through several window openings on either side of the steeply slanted roof, which gave a light and airy feel to the inn.

One of the Traders was eating from a steaming bowl of stew. A man and a woman were standing at the bar chatting with a woman on the other side of the counter. Three Traders, all from different villages, were talking at a table on the far side of the inn.

A man with an apron around his waist walked over to greet Joshua and his friends.

"Welcome to The Trader's Post. Can I get you kids something to eat?"

He led them over to an empty table. With a smile, he held a chair out for Sarah and everyone sat down. Pulling out a notepad and pencil from his breast pocket, he licked the tip of the pencil and held it poised above the notepad.

"Well, now," he went on, surveying the four of them each in turn, "where are you young folks from? No, no, don't tell me!" he added and smiled. "Let me see if I can guess."

He looked at each of them in turn again.

"We have...a young lady from Jemarrah, a Fixer if I'm not mistaken? Am I right?" he asked, grinning at Sarah and waiting for a response.

"Yes, that's right," Sarah said. She raised her brow at Joshua. The man smiled and seemed satisfied with himself. He next looked at Joshua and Andrew.

"And if I'm not mistaken, we have two young Woodsmen from...Morelle?" the pitch of his voice rose as he spoke the name of Joshua & Andrew's tribe, as if unsure of himself.

"That's right," Joshua said, also smiling. "How did you..."

"Oh, we get all sorts through here," the man interrupted. "You get to know the colours after a while. We don't get many folks from out west, mind you. Morelle is a long way from here. Have you been travelling for long?" Joshua and Andrew looked at each other.

"It certainly seems so," Joshua said nodding his head. The man next looked at Galleon, pursed his lips and tapped his pencil on his chin a few times.

"Hmmmm," he said with a slow exhale. "I do apologise. I'm normally very good at this. You're not from around here, that's for sure."

"I'm originally from the Southern Tip," Galleon said, putting the man out of his misery.

"Ah, well," the man said, beaming and tapping his pencil on the notepad. "We hardly ever see people from that far away."

"Um, what's the name of this village?" Joshua asked.

"Oh, welcome to Temerelle," the man said with a bow, "crossroads of the North. I'm Nedwell. Now, how about a nice cauldron of stew?"

He smiled and looked at each of them in turn, waiting to see who would respond.

"That sounds great," Joshua said after nodding at the others around the table. Everyone agreed and the pleasant waiter walked off, writing on his notepad.

"You never said you were from the Southern Tip." Andrew said to Galleon.

"You never asked."

Andrew raised his brow and shrugged his shoulders. "I guess that's a fair point."

"What else can you tell us about your people, Galleon?" Joshua asked. It occurred to him they had never really spoken much about where Galleon was from.

"Well," Galleon said raising his brow and exhaling, "there's not really that much to tell. My people come from the far south of Forestium near a place called the Southern Tip. We tend to keep pretty much to ourselves down there. Well, what I really mean by that is that we're a quarrelsome race, often getting into trouble with neighbouring villages. We're not always welcomed with open arms where we go, funny enough. My people are, by and large, a stubborn race, and there have been some terrible tribal wars in the past. I do have to say, though, I've been pleasantly surprised at how welcoming people get the farther away from the Southern Tip I go. As a matter of fact, I'm not even sure I want to go back home."

Galleon stared into nothingness and sighed. "I mean, there's really no reason for me to go back there as things currently stand." He looked around the table at the others. "I don't have a home left to go back to anyway."

"Well, maybe that will change when your people are freed?" Sarah suggested.

Galleon looked at her with a smile and shrugged.

Nedwell returned with a steaming cauldron of stew. He placed it in the centre of the table and laid out four settings of bowls and spoons. With a smile and a polite nod, he left them to tuck in.

When they had finished eating, Andrew and Galleon went over to the counter to see about getting rooms for the night.

Now that they were alone together, Sarah reached over and took Joshua's hand. Gazing into his eyes, she raised his hand, held it to her mouth and kissed it tenderly.

"I'm guessing it won't be long before we make it to Jemarrah."

"Hmmm," Sarah said smiling and nodding.

Her smile slowly faded.

"I can't stop thinking about what the Orb of Time showed you. My father never told me how my mother died."

Her face changed and she looked down at the table. Her smile had given way to a look of concern. Joshua gently lifted her head up with his finger under her chin and leaned forward.

"Don't worry," he whispered. "Whatever happens, we'll face it together."

Sarah smiled. She leaned over and they kissed.

The following morning, the four of them assembled in the inn again for breakfast. A Trader was at the counter telling Nedwell all about a new drink he had come across called Wood-wine. He had brought samples with him and the four of them chuckled to each other when Nedwell took a sip and didn't notice a golden froth of foam on his upper lip.

After breakfast, the four of them stood up to leave, and Nedwell came over to bid them farewell.

"Where are you young folks off to next?" he asked with a smile.

"Oh, we're heading back to my village, Jemarrah," Sarah said.

"Can you point us in the right direction?" Joshua asked.

"Jemarrah, eh?" Nedwell said tapping his chin with his pencil. "Well, it's easy enough to find. You turn left out of here and you keep on going. It's a few days travel. There aren't any other villages between here and there, so you shouldn't miss it."

Nedwell bid them a farewell and they were on their way.

A couple of hours after they left, a man with a hooded cloak hurried into the Trader's Post. It was Melachor. Despite carrying a steamy cauldron of stew, Nedwell rushed over and greeted him with a smile.

"Have you seen a group of young travellers around these parts?" Melachor demanded.

A Chirvel scurried about near one of the openings in the ceiling directly above. It screeched, and the noise made Nedwell jump, causing him to spill some of the hot stew onto Melachor.

"The young travellers," Melachor demanded, wiping his cloak. "Have you seen them?"

"We get lots of travellers through here," the apologetic host said, taking a step back and putting the cauldron onto a table. "They don't call Temerelle the crossroads of the North for nothing," he added with a sympathetic smile, joining Melachor in wiping his cloak.

"Two boys and a girl!" Melachor blurted, pushing Nedwell's hands away. "They were travelling with an Imp."

"Oh," Nedwell thought for a moment, "you mean that little fella from the Southern Tip? You've missed them. They left earlier this morning."

"Do you know where they were heading?" Melachor pleaded with wide eyes.

"Oh, well, let me think," Nedwell said tapping his pencil to his chin a couple of times. "Jemarrah, I think she said. Going back to her home village, they were. If you turn left out the door…"

Before Nedwell had finished the sentence, Melachor ran out of the inn, leaving the door swinging open behind him.

The Chirvel on the roof scurried down to the eave of the roof. It stood up on its hind legs and watched as Melachor disappeared down the path to the left. It ran back up to the top of the roof and stood on its hind legs. Two wings formed, and the creature grew in size as it morphed into a Raetheon. The huge bird flexed its white wings, lifted itself into the sky and flew off in the direction Melachor was running.

CHAPTER TWENTY-ONE

Melachor closes in

Melachor had made swift progress through the forest following the trail of the other four but he stopped by a thicket of Bramock bushes.

Hurriedly, he removed several of the inner stems and began fashioning them into arrows for his bow. Taking a piece of flint from inside his cloak, he struck with a rock a few times until several razor-sharp shards lay on the ground in front of him.

He carefully secured the sharpest of shards to the ends of each arrow. The shards were so sharp and his haste so great, he cut his fingers several times during the process.

He was breathing heavily, possessed by desperation. This would be the only way of saving his family's very lives, and his own as well. Everything hinged on his ability to stop Joshua from finding the third orb.

Finally satisfied his weapons were ready, he loaded an arrow into his bow. He looked around for a target and noticed a juvenile Raetheon resting on a branch high up in the canopy.

He took aim at the white bird and launched the arrow. It struck the poor beast directly in the heart with such force that the arrow sliced its way clean through and out the other side. The innocent bird never had a chance to make so much as a shriek.

The force of the arrow sent the Raetheon hurtling backwards, and it spiralled towards the ground with its wings flapping until it hit forest floor. It bounced on the leaf-litter and lay there motionless.

Melachor put his bow over his shoulder and loaded the remaining arrows into his quiver. He set off running at high speed, following the others.

Melachor was running like his life depended on it. He jumped over fallen logs and scratched his face on vines as he ran through thick vegetation. His haste was so great he barely had time to raise his hands to protect himself. Sweat was pouring down his face and his heart pounded.

He approached the edge of a clearing and thought he heard some noise ahead. Peering frantically through the remaining vegetation, he slowed down to a brisk walk, spotting Joshua and his other three companions out in the open.

Melachor stopped and ducked behind a thicket of Bramock bushes.

With a deep breath to steady himself, he took one of the flint-laden arrows and readied his bow, taking aim at Joshua. He carefully straightened up to get a clearer shot and pulled as hard as he could on the bowstring to the point it was cutting into his fingertips.

Just as he was about to release the arrow, there was an almighty roar, and a Wood-boar launched itself at him from just off to his left. The impact sent him flying to the ground.

The Wood-boar mauled at his face and its claws tore into his arms. Melachor rolled over on the ground and grappled with the ferocious animal. The wild beast bit at Melachor's throat and blood poured from multiple gaping wounds.

Melachor curled up into a ball, then lashed out at the forest creature. He eventually dislodged it by kicking at it with both feet. That sent the salivating beast rolling over several times.

It scrambled to its feet and stood there, growling back at him. Melachor managed to grab his bow. As he fumbled to load an arrow, the Wood-boar started to contort and change shape. In just a few seconds, it had morphed into a Raetheon. The Raetheon flexed its wings and took to the air towards Joshua and the others, who were running away in the opposite direction.

Melachor stood up, loaded the arrow and took aim. Blood was oozing from his neck and face, and he could barely see the fleeing Joshua past the Raetheon that was flying left and right through his line of sight.

Joshua looked over his shoulder and Melachor caught sight of his eyes. He pulled the bow back and released the arrow. It hurtled directly towards Joshua. The Raetheon swerved, and the arrow struck it with such force it tumbled forwards and fell to the ground.

The Raetheon let out a shriek of pain that echoed loudly in the clearing. It twisted and contorted as it changed shape several times. Joshua watched the Raetheon change to a Wood-boar then to a Woodsman and back to a shrieking Raetheon. The horrific wailing of unbearable pain continued to fill the air, as various body parts formed and reformed over and over. Shrieks and roars rang out throughout the clearing.

Eventually, the poor Metamorph collapsed into a heap on the ground. The various disjoined pieces of body parts slowly turned to dust, which floated into the air and were carried away by the wind. Melachor looked on in furious disappointment. With blood oozing onto his shirt he clutched at his neck to try to stem the bleeding. He turned, running off into the forest and out of sight.

Joshua and the others ran as fast as they could out of the clearing and continued at great speed for several more minutes before stopping to catch their breaths.

"W-what was that thing?" Andrew gasped, trying to catch his breath.

"I think…I think it was a Metamorph," Joshua said panting. "It could have been Protello. I don't know."

"Whoever or whatever it was," Galleon said taking several deep breaths and leaning forward with his hands on his knees, "I think it just saved your life, Joshua. That arrow was heading straight for you."

Joshua nodded. He was still panting and holding his hips.

"But who would want to kill you?" Sarah asked.

"Protello said another had been sent to stop me. That could have been who it was."

"Did you get a look at him?" Galleon asked.

Joshua shook his head.

"He was too far away. All I could see was the Raetheon being struck by something."

Christopher D. Morgan

CHAPTER TWENTY-TWO
Orb of Time-2

The encounter with the mystery adversary had shaken Joshua. It was bad enough someone had made an attempt on his life but he also worried he was putting his friends at great risk by his very presence. He felt an overwhelming need to do something. He wanted to know who was behind the attack, but it could have been anyone or indeed anything. He considered using the Orb of Vision, but judging by what happened when Galleon did so, that might lead the Goat directly to him, and he felt this to be too risky.

Joshua reached into his keeper bag and pulled out the Orb of Time.

"Just what do you think you're going to do with that?"

"I have to do something, Galleon. If the Goat has sent someone after me, I have to find out who it is. If I could just find out who was trying to attack me, it might help us."

"No!" Sarah gasped, holding her hands to her mouth. "It's too dangerous. And besides, you can't keep putting yourself through that kind of stress, Joshua."

Joshua looked Sarah in the eye. He knew she was right but he also knew he couldn't just wait for the attacker to strike again. The next time, he might not be so lucky. Worse still, he knew he could never live with himself if something happened to her or one of the others. Joshua hoped the Orb of Time might at least provide him with some clues to help him. He turned to Andrew.

"Don't do it," Andrew said, slowly shaking his head.

Joshua turned to his Imp friend. Galleon said nothing but shook his head and pursed his lips.

Joshua took a deep breath and looked down at the roll of cloth. He unwrapped the orb and peered into it.

There was a blinding flash and Joshua was floating and disconnected from his body once again. His heart pounded. It was the only sound he heard and it echoed through his mind.

There was a woman Joshua recognised as his mother sitting in a rocking chair. An infant child on her lap looked up at its mother and reached for her face. She looked down at the boy and kissed his tiny fingers.

A man entered the room and walked over to where she sat cradling the baby.

"Look," he said to Joshua's mother, holding up what looked like a mirror and showing it to her. "This is the Mirror of Prophecy. It will tell us what the future holds for our son."

Joshua's mother held his father's hand and smiled as he knelt beside her and gazed into her eyes. Joshua's father took the mirror and peered into it.

Joshua couldn't make out what it was his father saw in the mirror, but the Warrior's reaction was intense. His mouth opened and he wept as he continued to stare at the image.

At first, Joshua couldn't tell if those were tears of joy or sadness, but the Warrior started weeping even more. Joshua's father lowered the mirror and bent his head forward. He leaned towards his wife and she clasped her hands around the back of his neck with a worried look on her face.

"What is it?" she asked. "What did you see?"

With tears rolling down his face, he looked up and gazed into her eyes.

"Great pain and suffering," he said with a tremor in his voice.

Both of them looked down at the baby Joshua, still cradled in his mother's arms. The man's lip quivered as he stroked the infant's head.

Joshua looked on at the scene before him with a sense of helplessness difficult to endure. He wanted to reach out and comfort them both but there was another flash and the scene changed. It swirled into a vortex of clouds before fading altogether.

There was another blinding flash, and Joshua found himself looking at a young man. He was standing in a forest clearing, staring at the ground with his arms down by his sides.

The swirling image came into focus. Joshua's heartbeats pounded, and he could hear their rhythmic beating echo in his mind. He squinted and leaned forward. Could it be the mystery attacker he was trying to identify? He looked closer and leaned in still further until he realised he was looking at himself.

Joshua didn't recognise the event so he knew it had to be in the future, but he appeared to be the same age and was wearing the same clothing.

The future Joshua had a pale, blank expression. Tears were rolling down his cheeks and his puffy eyes were glazed over. Joshua squinted some more to try to make out the rest of the scene. As far as he could tell, there was nobody else present. He tried to see what it was the future Joshua was staring down at.

As the image continued to come into focus, Joshua was horrified to see it was a grave. The future Joshua was standing over somebody's grave, but he couldn't see whose it was. There was no tombstone; just a long mound of freshly dug earth. Whoever it was had just been buried.

Thoughts of dread raced through Joshua's mind, but then the future Joshua appeared to speak very softly.

"I'm sorry," he murmured with a tremor. The sound of his own grief-stricken voice frightened him.

"I tried my best, but it was not good enough."

"Joshua! JOSHUA!" Sarah was screaming at him and shaking his shoulders.

"Joshua, please!"

Joshua blinked several times and slowly came around.

"What? Who? Where am I?"

Slowly becoming aware of his surroundings, Joshua found Sarah standing right in front of him. Was it her? Had that been Sarah's grave he was standing over? The toll this was taking on Joshua's emotions was enormous, and he broke into floods of tears. He threw his arms around her and she held him tightly.

"No," he cried as he clung to her, "please no, don't let it be true!"

Sarah caressed him and patted him on his back.

"Shhhh," she whispered into his ear, swaying with him gently side to side, "I'm here. Everything will be all right now, shhhh."

She too began weeping as they continued their embrace. His experience with the Orb of Time had again reduced him to a complete emotional wreck, and all Sarah could do was to hold on to him.

Andrew and Galleon looked at each other but neither of them knew what they could do to help ease the pain.

CHAPTER TWENTY-THREE
Orb of Vision-2

Joshua was still shaking from his experience with the Orb of Time for some time afterwards, and felt too tired to travel very far. The others found a secluded spot in the forest and set up camp for the night.

The mood around the campfire was sombre. Joshua said nothing and just sat there thinking about what he should do next. Sarah sat beside him clutching his hand to her chest. He felt comforted by the warmth of her touch but found himself unable to shake the thought that it might have been her grave in the vision. Clinging to her hand now made him feel she was safe even if that wasn't actually the case.

More than ever, Joshua wanted to find out who made the attempt on his life and why. Protello had told him the Goat had sent someone to stop him. Maybe if he could talk to the Goat, he might learn the truth.

Perhaps an encounter with the Orb of Vision would bring him the answers he needed, he thought to himself. Galleon had two encounters with the Goat and he seemed no worse for it. What harm could it do?

Joshua looked around the campfire at the others. He felt a great sense of responsibility for them and decided it was time to act.

"I'm going to talk to the Goat," he announced.

Sarah sat up straight and shook her head. "No, Joshua, you can't!"

"Are you mad?" Andrew yelled.

"It's too dangerous!" Galleon added. "What do you hope to achieve by doing that, anyway? You know the Goat is on the lookout for you and the last thing you want is to reveal your whereabouts to Him."

Joshua stood up and paced around the fire. The others watched him as he moved around staring at the floor.

"Look, it's bad enough the Goat has sent someone to kill me, but it's putting all of you in danger too. How could I live with myself if something happened to any of you?"

Andrew stood up and looked Joshua in the eye, and said, "We're in this together. And besides, what makes you think the Goat's going to tell you anything anyway?"

Joshua felt he didn't have the mental energy to argue the point with them all. He decided he needed to clear his mind and started walking off into the forest.

"Joshua, where are you going?" Sarah asked.

He turned and looked at her. He paused before turning to the fire and said in a calm voice, "We need more Flame-bark. I'll go and find some. The walk will help me clear my mind."

"I'll go with you," Andrew said, walking towards him.

"No, it's OK," Joshua said, holding up his hand and facing it to Andrew. "I just…I just need to be alone for a while. I'll be fine, really."

He turned and headed into the forest to find more Flame-bark. Sarah started after him but Andrew caught her eye and shook his head.

"Just give him a bit of space," he said to her softly. "He'll be fine."

Sarah watched Joshua disappear and then, after a moment's pause, sat down by the fire again. She picked up his weapon belt and clutched it to her chest. She looked at Andrew and Galleon with puffy eyes and shook her head.

"I don't know how much more of this he can take."

Galleon moved over to sit beside her. He put his arm gently around her shoulder.

"Don't worry. Joshua is stronger than you know. I think he's handling it all really very well."

He looked at Andrew and nodded with widened eyes. Picking up on Galleon's cue, he smiled and nodded back towards Sarah.

"He's strong," Andrew said. "I've seen this in him before. He just needs to clear his head. Don't worry. He'll be back before you know it."

Galleon comforted Sarah with his arm around her shoulder and they sat there gazing into the fire.

Joshua wandered around in the forest aimlessly for a few minutes. He didn't stray so far that he couldn't see the flickering light from the fire, but he wasn't having much luck locating any Flame-bark.

It was getting dark and the thick, humid air was coming alive with the sound of Dengles. Joshua loved the humming sound they made. It was reassuring in a way that it always reminded him of home and filled him with happy thoughts.

As he strode around, trying to avoid the prickly vines and low-hanging branches, he watched the ground, trying not to lose his step but also trying to look for Flame-bark.

Then he stopped and looked up. From the corner of his eye he glimpsed a pair of eyes staring at him. Joshua froze mid-stride. He slowly turned his head in that direction. Just off to his left, sitting on a low-hanging branch was a Wood-boar. It was a good-sized beast, at least as big as Joshua. Sharp claws gripped the branch it was perched on, and its fangs dripped with saliva. The hairy beast was looking directly at him.

Joshua reached for his slingshot, but his belt and weapon were back at the camp. His terror soared as he realised he was weaponless. He thought of making a dash for it back to the campfire, but there was thick vegetation all around and a fully grown Wood-boar would be too quick to outrun.

He considered his options but none of them seemed appealing. A scream for help would attract the attention of the others, but that would also startle the wild animal and by the time they arrived, he could easily be dead.

Joshua's heart skipped a beat, and he took a sharp intake of breath as the Wood-boar leaned forward and jumped to the ground. But before it had time to land, it morphed into the figure of a Woodsman. Joshua gazed with open jaw as Protello walked up to him and put his hand on his shoulder.

"It's OK, my friend," the Metamorph said in a soft tone. "You're safe."

For several moments, Joshua was unable to speak.

"I…I thought you were dead. I…I saw you killed."

"That was another of my kind. The man that shot at you was injured but he is still alive."

Joshua looked at his friend with wide eyes.

"Who was he?" he asked.

"His name is Melachor. He is trying to prevent you from finding the third orb. He is trying to kill you, Joshua, and he will stop at nothing to prevent you from fulfilling your destiny."

Joshua paced back and forth and shook his head.

"No, no, that doesn't make sense. Melachor traded the Orb of Vision with me to begin with. He was desperate, but the poor man just wanted to get his hands on the Mirror of Prophecy to find out what happened to his family. If he wanted to kill me, he could easily have done it after the trade. Why would he be trying to stop me from finding the third orb?"

"He is not acting of his own accord. The Goat commands him now. He fears the Goat and there is nobody more skilful at manipulating fear than the Goat."

Joshua continued to pace back and forth, scratching his head.

"Why is he so afraid of the Goat? What control does He have over him?"

The Metamorph shook his head. Joshua paced some more. His mind was racing again.

"If only I could find out what it is that makes Melachor so afraid of the Goat maybe I could convince him otherwise."

Joshua stopped and looked over to where the campfire was flickering in the distance. He could just about see Sarah sitting and clutching his belt. If Melachor was to make another attempt on his life, it might be her or one of the others that got hurt instead of himself. Joshua knew he had to prevent that from happening. He turned to Protello.

"Galleon said he could sense the Goat's thoughts when he experienced the Orb of Vision. Is that how it works?"

"The Orb of Vision opens a gateway to the Goat's mind. But beware. The connection works both ways, Joshua. You must be cautious. The Goat has incredible discipline of thought and is a skilful manipulator. You will do well to distinguish what is real and what the Goat wants you to see."

Joshua scratched his chin as he took in Protello's advice.

"I must leave you now, my friend. I will try to find Melachor again."

Protello walked away.

"Wait! The other Metamorph? Who was it?"

Protello looked down at the ground in front of him and sighed, turning back to Joshua again.

"Malena was my soulmate. Do not let her death be in vain, Joshua. Bring the orbs together and open the Portallas!"

Protello took a step back. Wings extended from his shoulders. Within seconds, he morphed into a Raetheon and flew off into the dark forest. Joshua followed the Raetheon with his gaze until it was out of sight, then he turned and headed back to the campfire.

Sarah stood up as he arrived. She was still clutching his belt.

"Are you OK, Joshua?" Galleon asked him.

"I'm going to use the Orb of Vision to talk to the Goat."

Sarah gasped and Galleon stood up. Andrew opened his mouth to say something but Joshua cut him off.

"It's no use trying to talk me out of it, either. Melachor is still out there somewhere and he's looking for me. If I can find out what it is the Goat has over him, maybe I can do something about it and stop him. That way," he went on with a softer tone, "that way, you'll all be safer."

Joshua walked over to Sarah and put his hands on her shoulders. He looked into her eyes and spoke softly. "I can't let anything happen to you."

Sarah put her arms around him in a warm embrace. It lingered for a few moments before he let her go.

"Now," he said, turning to Galleon, "I'll be able to read the Goat's thoughts, right?"

"Yes, but He'll be able to read your thoughts too, and control them."

"Hopefully, it won't last long enough for that. All I need is to understand why Melachor is so afraid of him. Once I have that information, I'll try to break the link."

Joshua picked up his keeper bag and pulled out the Orb of Vision, still wrapped in cloth. He looked at the others in turn, then unwrapped the orb and peered into it.

As he stared, the noise of the fire faded and Joshua could hear the sound of his breathing echoing through his mind. A murky, dark image formed inside the orb.

Joshua felt himself floating in a dark room, disconnected from his body. The image of the Goat formed before him. It was twisted and evil looking. The young man could sense pure hatred rushing through his thoughts. The Goat's dark eyes moved from side to side and Joshua sensed He was trying to figure out where their camp was. A wave of frustration engulfed him. The Goat fixed his gaze directly on Joshua.

Joshua's anxiety heightened as he thought this, and at once a hideous grin spread across the Goat's face. Joshua knew he had to discipline his mind and tried to empty it of thoughts.

"You are scared of me," the Goat snarled. Although His lips weren't moving, Joshua could sense the Goat's thoughts.

"Good. You should be."

Joshua found his thoughts racing with images, but not of his own doing. A jumble of disconnected sounds and events flooded his mind. The Goat was searching for something. He was testing Joshua's reaction to each image He was communicating. Joshua fought to ignore them, but the Goat's power was intense and Joshua felt powerless to resist.

Joshua felt a rush of grief when he saw an image of Sarah feeling sad. The Goat's smile widened. Without warning, the same image of his future self standing over the grave flooded his mind. He tried hard to push it to one side, but it persisted and he couldn't shake it no matter how much he tried to concentrate.

In his mind, he looked down at the grave but it seemed somehow different to how he remembered it. There was now a tombstone present at one end of the long mound of earth. Powerless to resist his own thoughts, Joshua felt himself staring hard at the inscription on the tombstone. It read 'RIP Sarah, my dearest love.' A wave of uncontrollable grief gripped him with such intensity he felt it would tear him apart from the inside.

Joshua's emotions overwhelmed him. His grief turned to anger, and then to rage. He looked at the Goat's malevolent face. Exerting his own will, his mind turned to the Orb of Suffering. He needed to get the third orb to open the Portallas.

Fear flooded his thoughts. Joshua sensed it was not his own fear but the Goat's. Uncontrolled terror raced through Joshua's mind. He saw Melachor whimpering on the floor in the corner. The image lasted briefly before being replaced by another of Melachor being gripped by his throat at the Goat's hands. 'Stop the boy or your family will die,' rang in his ears.

Joshua closed his eyes and concentrated as intensely as he had ever done before. At that moment the orb fell from his hand and his legs went weak. As he collapsed, Andrew and Sarah caught him and lowered him gently to the ground. He slowly opened his eyes and looked around. The sight of Andrew, Sarah and Galleon looking down at him came into focus.

"Joshua? Are you OK?" Sarah asked.

It took a few moments before he realised he was lying on the forest floor by the campfire. He raised his hands and Sarah and Andrew lifted him to his feet.

"It's his family. The Goat has Melachor's family and He's using them to get to him. That's why he's so afraid of Him. That's why he'll do anything to stop me. He fears the Goat will kill his wife and children."

"What else did you see?" Galleon asked.

Joshua looked at Sarah. A wave of sadness gripped him again and tears began welling in his eyes. Sarah looked him in the eye and saw real fear staring back at her. She threw her arms around him and held him tightly. Joshua rested his head on her shoulder and cried. She gently cradled the back of his head and the two of them stood there holding each other.

Christopher D. Morgan

CHAPTER TWENTY-FOUR

Isabelle

It was another full day of travel before the four of them reached the outskirts of Jemarrah. Sarah's bubbly enthusiasm was returning.

"It's not far now. My sister and I used to climb that tree when we were young. Oh, the fun we used to have throwing Yucust cones at unsuspecting Traders passing by."

"I bet you're looking forward to seeing everyone again." Galleon said. Sarah's faced beamed and she spun around with her arms outstretched.

"Oh, I can't wait! Once we cross the stream up ahead, you'll see Jemarrah. It's a wonderful place. I really think you'll like it there."

Joshua recognised the tunic colours of some of the Woodsmen they encountered but not all of them. A few were from the same tribe he had seen during the vision with the Orb of Time but there seemed to be Woodsmen from all over Forestium here.

As they walked, a young woman about Sarah's age approached them. Judging by her uniform, she was a Jemarrah Tender. She stopped a few paces in front of them and stared, tilting her head forward and squinting.

"Sarah?" she said, tilting her head forward some more and widening her eyes.

"Sarah, is that you?"

Sarah beamed with delight and the two of them ran towards each other. They threw their arms around each other, screaming joyfully.

"It is you," she repeated several times, as the two girls jumped excitedly up and down and hugged.

"I can't believe it. I thought you'd never return to us. You've been gone far too long. You must have learned heaps, though."

Sarah smiled from ear to ear and nodded enthusiastically.

"Ahem," Andrew said.

"Oh," Sarah said and turning to the others, "some introductions are in order. I want you all to meet my sister, Isabelle."

Joshua, Andrew and Galleon all smiled and waved in unison.

"This is Galleon…and Joshua" Sarah motioned to them in turn.

She reached out, grabbed Joshua's hand and pulled him towards her, then beamed at Isabelle.

Joshua opened his mouth but didn't seem able to produce any words, so he just smiled. The two girls looked at each other and giggled in unison. Isabelle raised her brow and nodded at Sarah. She pointed her thumb upwards just in front of her chest where the others couldn't see.

"And this," Sarah said, turning to Andrew, "this…is Joshua's best friend…Andrew."

Isabelle looked Andrew up and down. Her eyes widened as she surveyed slowly from top to bottom and back to top again. Andrew shifted uncomfortably on his feet and his face reddened. Isabelle looked back at Sarah and they both giggled again, shrugging their shoulders and raising their eyebrows at each other.

"Come Sarah, we must celebrate your return at once."

The five of them walked on towards Jemarrah. Sarah and Isabelle were holding hands and joyfully telling each other all about what happened over the past several months. Despite her enthusiasm and attention to Isabelle, Sarah didn't once let go of Joshua's hand.

Every now and then, Isabelle would turn to look over her shoulder at Andrew and the two sisters would giggle like giddy schoolgirls. It made Andrew blush each time, and this just seemed to add to their sense of amusement. Galleon nudged

Andrew to attract his attention. Andrew leaned down to hear what he had to say.

"Don't worry, I'm sure she'll warm up to you eventually." The mischievous Imp said with a chuckle. Andrew gave him a friendly shove that almost knocked him off his feet and shook his head dismissively with a reddened face.

As they neared the town they noticed more and more signs of civilisation. Joshua and Andrew looked around with wide eyes. Even though they had not yet reached the centre, it already looked to be a much bigger place than Morelle.

Joshua and Andrew had only ever seen smaller, neighbouring villages in the west of Forestium. Neither of them had seen any place as big as this.

The first dwellings they saw seemed very similar to the huts they were familiar with from Morelle, but there were also some strange-looking buildings wrapped entirely around trees. Above these, Joshua was amazed to see odd wooden constructions built around the trees high up in the air. Huge tree trunks branched out from them as if the tree had grown through the middle of a hut and lifted it clear into the air. Rope ladders stretched between the buildings on the ground and those in the air, and walkways crisscrossed beneath the treetop canopy linking the trees together.

"What are those?" Joshua said with wide eyes and pointing up into the treetops.

"What, those?" Sarah said, following Joshua's line of sight. "Oh, those are lookout posts. They were abandoned many years ago. Screechers used to use them to watch for marauders but nobody uses them anymore."

"Screechers?" Andrew asked.

"Screechers," Isabelle explained, turning to him, "were people who stood watch and raised the alarm if they saw attacking tribes approaching from the South. I've heard the Elder talk about them before."

Andrew's jaw hung open as he kept gawking at the walkways and cabins high up in the trees.

"We don't have anything like this where we come from," Joshua said. He too was shaking his head and gazing up at the structures above him.

"My village isn't nearly as big as this. I've heard of stories of tribal wars from long ago but that's all in the past, I suppose. We don't have any need for lookouts or anything like that."

"Neither do we, really. Not anymore, that is. The tribal wars ended many years ago. Nowadays, Jemarrah is home to people from many different tribes and we all live in harmony. It's better that way, don't you think? Hardly anyone ever goes up there to the lookout posts anymore."

"Except for when you've broken your mother's favourite cauldron and are trying to find a great place to hide," Sarah said, looking at Isabelle, who was cringing and grinning from ear to ear. Both the girls burst into fits of laughter.

Joshua was thrilled to see Sarah having such fun. It lifted his spirits and he was starting to relax, himself.

Isabelle insisted she prepare them all a nice, home-cooked meal, to which everyone agreed.

"I should visit father first," Sarah suggested to Isabelle when they arrived at her hut.

"Oh, you can't. The Elder won't be back for at least another day."

"More trials?"

"Well, you know, Jemarrah. The place has gotten so big that rarely a month goes past without a new group of hopefuls setting off to do their stupid trials. The Elder has even started taking young Woodsmen from other tribes with him. There must have been more than twenty of them this time around."

Joshua and Andrew listened to this with particular interest. It would be a true honour for any Woodsman to participate in the trials in the presence of a village Elder. With Morelle's Elder being so old and frail, that was never going to be possible for either of them. It wasn't hard to see why Woodsmen from other tribes might be attracted to Jemarrah with such a vibrant and active village Elder able to participate in the trials with them.

"Welcome to my humble abode," Isabelle announced as they arrived at her modest hut and she led them in.

Isabelle's home was small but comfortable. The main living room behind the front door was decorated with lots of flowers and other plants. Most were arranged in an assortment of pots and vases placed in every nook and cranny. Some hung from the rafters. No shelf was left empty and no floor space unused. The clutter and pleasant floral odour made it feel homely.

Off from the living room was a tiny kitchen. Judging by the herbs, spices and other ingredients hanging there, Isabelle shared Sarah's enthusiasm for cooking. The kitchen led through to a bedroom at the back. In the main living room a couple of comfortable sofas in front of an open fire looked inviting.

Once everyone was inside, the girls caught up with all the latest gossip, whilst Isabelle prepared them all a hearty Jemarrah feast.

Sarah told her all about the various Shrooms and berries she had learned about and how she had prepared grassland Flarrets with little more than a campfire and wild grasses. Isabelle listened intently and kept raising her eyebrows each time Sarah mentioned something she'd learned.

The two girls continued to prepare the food in the kitchen, whilst Joshua, Andrew and Galleon sat and rested.

"So, tell me," Isabelle whispered to Sarah when the two of them were alone in the kitchen. "This Andrew friend of yours; does he, um, you know, does he…have someone waiting for him back home?"

The two girls giggled.

"I don't know. Maybe you should ask him? Don't tell me you still haven't found love?"

Isabelle shrugged her shoulders.

"And your handsome friend, Joshua?" she asked raising her eyebrows. "You clearly like him a lot. Is he, um, well, you know…"

She was stirring the cauldron but kept glancing briefly at Sarah. The pot was starting to steam with all the delicious-smelling ingredients she had added to it.

"Well, I mean, do you think, maybe…he's the one?"

Her tone rose towards the end of the question, and she paused, looking Sarah in the eye. Sarah smiled. She bent over the steamy cauldron of stew and sniffed.

"Hmmm. Lovely stew. Shall we eat?"

With that, she picked up the cauldron, looked at Isabelle and winked. Both girls laughed again and went into the next room with the hot cauldron of stew.

Galleon and the boys stood up when the girls entered the room, and they all took a place at the table. Sarah sat next to Joshua. She took his hand, squeezed it and smiled at him.

"So, Galleon, wasn't it?" Isabelle said, passing bowls and spoons around the table. "Sarah tells me you're from the South?"

"Um, that's right," he replied. He kept his gaze on the steaming cauldron in the middle of the table. "I'm, um, from a village not far from the Southern Tip."

"Well," Isabelle said raising her brow, "you *are* a very long way from home."

She heaped generous portions of stew into everyone's bowls and they all tucked in.

"You're the second Imp we've seen here in Jemarrah in recent months." She filled her own bowl last and took a seat. Galleon had stopped eating and perked up, as did the others, including Sarah. Everyone was now staring at Isabelle.

"You've…you've seen another Imp?" Galleon asked with raised eyebrows.

"What, here in Jemarrah?" he added.

Isabelle took a spoonful of stew and blew on it. She took a sip of the soup and looked up to see everyone staring at her.

"Well, yes. Why? What's wrong?"

"I've been searching for many years throughout Forestium looking for other Imps. I was beginning to think I was the last of my kind."

"I don't ever remember there being an Imp here in Jemarrah," Sarah said to Isabelle, tilting her head and raising an eyebrow.

"Lilly arrived not long after you left a few months ago."

"Lilly? Her name's Lilly? Do you know her?" Galleon asked.

"Well, sure, I know her. She's, um…all sorts of fun."

Galleon sat up straight and looked around the table before his gaze landed back on Isabelle again. A smile began to stretch across his face.

"Well, where is she? Is she here? Can I meet her?"

"Well, I don't see why not. But…um," Isabelle looked at Galleon and then at the others around the table.

"Look, it's just a suggestion but, um, it might be a good idea for you all to...clean up a bit first?"

She raised her pitch and eyebrow at the end of that suggestion and put on a false grin. "I mean, you kind of look like you've crawled backwards through a Wood-boar hole."

They all looked at each other. Their hair was matted and untidy and their clothes and faces were muddy. There was a pause and then everyone laughed.

Galleon talked about the prospect of meeting another Imp all the way through the rest of the meal. Joshua thought he was overloading poor Isabelle with endless questions but she did the best she could to keep up with him and took it all in her stride. Galleon was so excited; he kept saying how keen he was to make a good first impression when they went to meet with Lilly in the morning.

Isabelle offered them all the opportunity to clean up and stay the night, but Galleon noticed there was only space for about four people to sleep, so he suggested he would freshen up and stay the night at an inn instead.

Isabelle had been eyeing Andrew all evening. When Galleon announced he was heading over to the inn, Andrew looked decidedly uncomfortable.

"Um, maybe I should go with you?"

"That's OK, Andrew, there's plenty of space for you here if Galleon isn't staying."

Joshua chuckled to himself at Andrew's reddening face.

Galleon bid them all farewell and wandered over to a nearby inn for the night.

Joshua, Andrew and Sarah took turns having a hot bath and freshening up. Joshua thought Sarah looked even more radiant with her hair neatly brushed and tied up at the back. Her entire face was visible for the first time and it looked just perfect.

Once they were all settled around the open fire Andrew had lit, Joshua told Isabelle all about his dream and how he was hoping to find his father alive.

Sarah and Joshua cuddled up to each other and held hands. Isabelle sat on her own but she squeezed hard up to the end of the couch she was sitting on, leaving a suspiciously Andrew-sized spot next to her.

With Joshua and Sarah occupying the only other couch, this left nowhere else for him to sit, and Isabelle kept glancing at him and patting the seat next to her.

For his part Joshua's best friend kept busying himself with prodding and poking the fire.

Sarah and Joshua cast each other a sideways glance when Isabelle looked at Andrew and patted the cushion next to her. They giggled quietly to each other every time this happened, which just seemed to add to Andrew's embarrassment.

Joshua didn't want to say too much about his experiences with the orbs and the visions he had seen. He also avoided talking about the Goat and His intentions. For one thing, he didn't want to drag Isabelle into his plight for fear of putting her at risk. He also wanted to shield her from the burden of some of the truths he carried.

Besides this, he was also very relaxed and he hadn't felt this way for some time. He just wanted to revel in the comfort of not having to think about it all, even if only for a short while.

"I should get some more logs for the fire," Andrew suggested, despite there being plenty to choose from already.

"Oh, let me show you where they are," Sarah said.

She stood up and led Andrew out the back to find some more fire logs. Joshua sat upright on his couch and looked into the smouldering fire. Isabelle looked at him with a smile.

"You really like Sarah, don't you, Joshua."

Joshua looked at her and smiled. It was the sort of involuntary smile that gives away true feelings whether you want to or not.

"She's...she's truly amazing," he said with a big grin and a chuckle. "I've never met anyone like her. I mean, I only have to look at her and, well..."

Isabelle maintained eye contact with a smile.

"You really do care for her, don't you?" she murmured, nodding her head.

Joshua smiled again and nodded. His smile lingered for a moment before he turned to the fire and thought again of the vision he had of Sarah's name on the tombstone. His smile slowly faded and he stared into empty space. The thought of Sara's grave weighed so heavily on his mind, he could barely concentrate on anything else.

"Why are you so sad, Joshua?"

"I'm sorry," he shook his head, snapping himself out of his trance, "I don't mean to be rude. So tell me. You're about the same age as Sarah?"

Isabelle chuckled. "I'm actually a few years older but thanks, anyway. I'm not actually her sister either. I was adopted when I was a baby, but Sarah and I grew up together like sisters. Like many people from Jemarrah, I'm not originally from here."

Her smile widened. She took a deep breath and let out a sigh.

"Sarah's mother died when we were very young. Neither of us has any other brothers or sisters and so we're the closest thing we each have to family. Except for the Elder, of course. He's

211

been just as much a father to me as he has to Sarah. She and I have been getting into mischief with each other since we were old enough to pick Shrooms. I know her better than she knows herself."

Joshua's thoughts turned to his vision of when Sarah's mother was killed. His eyes began welling up. There was a long pause as he looked into nothingness.

"She was only a baby when it happened," he whispered.

Isabelle studied him. She said nothing but leaned forward and rested her chin on her hands.

"He never meant for it to happen," he said, shaking his head, his tone apologetic. "He never meant to kill her."

A tear formed in his eye as sadness gripped him. Isabelle got up, went to sit beside him and took his hand. She clasped it securely in hers and smiled gently.

"You know how Sarah's mother died?"

With a tear running down his cheek, he nodded.

"I saw it in a vision. It was my father. They were fighting: my father and Sarah's."

Joshua relived the moments he had endured seeing in the Orb of Time. Grief overwhelmed him again.

"It was an accident," he said, weeping without restraint.

"It's OK, Joshua," she said softly. "It wasn't your fault. It was a long time ago."

"I can't let anything happen to her," he said shaking his head and thinking about the tombstone again. "I have to protect her now."

He looked at the fire and took a deep breath.

"I have to protect her," he said, wiping his eyes with both hands.

Andrew and Sarah came back into the room, each with an armful of logs. They were laughing and joking with each other. Joshua finished wiping his eyes and made himself busy with loading some logs into the fire. Neither Sarah nor Andrew noticed what had just happened, and Isabelle never revealed it to them either.

Christopher D. Morgan

CHAPTER TWENTY-FIVE

Last of the Imps

The following morning, Joshua was the first to wake. He and Andrew had spent the night on the couches, whilst Sarah and Isabelle took the two beds.

Joshua didn't get up straight away. He spent some time lying there and thinking about what he had to do. According to Isabelle, the Elder might not be back for another day, so it didn't seem like there was much he could do for now.

He knew time was against him. To make matters worse, he was worried Melachor was still on the loose and probably looking for them. Joshua took comfort in at least knowing he was in a larger town now. He could blend in more easily. That would make it more difficult for Melachor to track him down, he hoped. Joshua hadn't seen any Blood-bats anywhere in Jemarrah so far, but he knew they could be lurking just about anywhere.

When Isabelle and Sarah walked in from the bedroom, Joshua got up. He nudged Andrew to wake him. Andrew was lying close to the edge of the couch and the shock of being woken was enough to dislodge him. He fell to the floor with a thump and looked around confused to find himself there, much to Sarah's and Isabelle's amusement.

"Come on, Sarah," Isabelle said laughing, "let's see if we can find these boys something to eat."

The two girls went out into the woods to find some breakfast. They walked to one of Isabelle's favourite spots not far from her hut and set about picking some early season Wood-shrooms.

They found a lovely cluster of ripened Shrooms near the base of an Ashfer and both bent down to slice them away.

"You're very lucky, Sarah," Isabelle proclaimed, as she sliced a big bunch of Shrooms from the base of the tree.

"What, me? Why's that?"

Isabelle stood upright and looked at her.

"Joshua, I mean."

She spoke with a deliberate tone. Sarah stood up and looked at her. Both girls smiled at each other. Sarah nodded and burst into tears. Both girls hugged.

"Thank you, thank you, thank you, Isabelle. Oh, it means so much to me that you like him."

After breakfast, they all went over to the inn to find Galleon so Isabelle could introduce him to Lilly. They found him sitting at one of the tables outside the inn with a half-empty bowl of Twiggling broth in front of him.

Joshua barely recognised Galleon in his clean clothes and neatly combed hair. He sported a new tunic and had polished his boots to a high sheen.

"Well, what do you think?"

Galleon stood up, extended his arms sideways and slowly turned around.

"Going somewhere special?" Andrew asked with a chuckle.

"Honestly! Laugh all you want but I haven't seen another of my kind for over ten years and I want to make the very best first impression. So, what do you think?"

216

"I think you look very handsome," Sarah exclaimed with a smile. "Lilly will be sure to find you very charming. Don't you think, Isabelle?"

Isabelle scratched the side of her head. She looked at Sarah with an enigmatic smile but said nothing. Sarah looked puzzled.

Joshua was starting to suspect there might be something Isabelle had not yet revealed about Lilly. Galleon bounced up and down on his heels, rubbing his palms together, and they set off into the village.

As they walked down the main path towards the village centre, Joshua kept casting sideways glances. Something didn't seem right. At first, he just thought it was his unfamiliarity with this new place, but he sensed there was something more to it, and this heightened his sense of unease.

There was plenty of bustling activity. Children were running about playing, and Traders in different colours walked back and forth. Rays of morning sunshine streamed through the treetop canopy. The shards of light illuminated the morning patches of mist drifting eerily between the buildings. Chirvels scurried about up and down the thatched roofs of the various buildings. Could any of those be a Metamorph?

A Raetheon was shrieking somewhere high above. He looked up, but couldn't see the bird through the bright streams of sunlight. Each time he heard a different sound, he looked quickly in that direction.

He noticed a Trader with a long, black overcoat. His beard was scruffy and untidy and he was straining to carry the weight of a brown sack over his shoulder. Joshua thought the Trader might be following them, but when he caught the man's eye, he turned away and walked off. Was he being paranoid? He caught Andrew's eye and the two of them exchanged glances.

"I feel it too," Andrew murmured.

Something was amiss, but Joshua couldn't quite put his finger on what it was.

"Here we are," Isabelle said, as they reached one of the larger log huts in the centre of the village.

It had a steeply slanted roof covered with thatches of straw. Several small openings were dotted about the roof and a small child was peering through one of them.

Two Chirvels stood up on their hind legs on the roof's apex and peered around looking for Raetheons. A waist-height thicket hedge encircled the rickety, wooden building, and there were children's toys scattered on the ground inside the fence.

To one side of a hole in the hedge was a post made from a twisted branch of an Ashfer tree. From it hung an uneven, wooden sign held up by a couple of pieces of vine. The board swayed gently in the breeze and the word "School" was carved onto it.

"Shall we, um, go inside?" Isabelle said to the others.

Without waiting for an answer, she walked through the gate and the others followed her, with Galleon the last through.

Isabelle pushed the front door open, and they all went in. Inside, there were no children, but a short, plump woman was sweeping the floor at the back of the room.

"Um...Lilly?" Isabelle called out across the empty hall. The woman stopped what she was doing and looked over her shoulder. She laid her broom against the wall and waddled over. She looked up at Isabelle and smiled.

"Hello, Lilly, I want to introduce you to some friends of mine," Isabelle said in a tentative tone. "This is Sarah, the sister I told you about? You remember? Sarah has been travelling and has just returned to Jemarrah."

Lilly smiled at Sarah and nodded.

"This is Joshua and Andrew. And this," she said as Joshua and Andrew stood aside to reveal Galleon standing there with a beaming smile and his hands behind his back, his head held high, "this…is Galleon."

Lilly looked at the short man and her smile disappeared.

"Um, h-hello, Lilly," Galleon stammered.

Lilly looked at him with a blank stare.

"And just what in the world do ya' 'tink ya' gawking at?" Lilly scoffed.

Galleon's smile faded. Isabelle cringed.

"Um…what?" he asked.

His eyes shifted over to Isabelle and he raised his eyebrows at her.

"Ya' heard me, ya' bleedin' fool. Don't just stand there wit' ya' mouth open looking like ya' 'tree berries short of a Bramock bush! Years it's taken me to get as far as away from d' bleedin' Southern Tip as possible. Just when I 'tought I'd found myself a quiet little corner all to m'self, ya' show up and are fixing to ruin it for me."

Joshua noticed Andrew pursing his lips together and just managing to hold back a chuckle. Andrew's eyes widened and he looked up and away.

"Um, well, it's just that, um…"

Joshua had never seen Galleon so lost for words.

Andrew bent down and whispered into his ear. "Don't worry, I'm sure she'll warm up to you eventually."

Galleon frowned at him. Andrew straightened up, quickly looking away.

"Right, Lilly," Galleon began tentatively, "when was the last time you actually saw another Imp?"

"Not nearly long enough!" she shouted. She underscored the point with a definitive nod. "Nothing but trouble, if ya' ask me, the lot of 'em!"

"You and I," Galleon persisted, "are likely the very last Imps in all of Forestium, Lilly."

She looked at him and then looked at the others in turn. "Is that so?" she said, rolling her eyes. "Well, just so long as ya' don't go getting any ideas, then!"

Andrew again tried to hold back a chuckle, although this time he didn't quite manage to hold it in.

Before Galleon could get another word in, Isabelle said, "Do you know what, Lilly? Why don't we all go and have a nice cup of tea or something?"

"Or maybe some'ting wit' a bit more bite to it." Lilly insisted. "Come on," she added, "and keep an eye on 'im! I don't want 'im getting any ideas."

By the time they left, Andrew was nearly in tears and barely able to keep his laughter contained.

CHAPTER TWENTY-SIX
The Elder Returns

Lilly led them over to the inn where Galleon had stayed the night before. As she walked in, she caught the eye of the man behind the counter.

"Pitcher of 'dat newfangled Wood-wine please, Feldo." she shouted.

For a newcomer, Joshua thought Lilly had no problems giving orders. Feldo nodded back and reached for some mugs hanging above the bar. The six friends found a large, round table, and all sat down around it.

Feldo brought a pitcher of the Wood-wine over to where they were sitting and poured each of them a mug full of the golden liquid.

"Here, some'ting new from down south," Lilly said.

"Oh, I've heard about this," Isabelle said, raising her eyebrows and clapping, "people all over have been talking about it. I've been meaning to try it myself."

Andrew and Galleon sniffed at their mugs and huge grins spread across their faces. Isabelle took one sip and nearly spat it out again, scrunching up her face and shaking her head.

"Oh, that's truly awful."

Lilly chuckled and everyone else took a mouthful. They all laughed as each of them licked the golden froth from their top lips.

"Now," Lilly said to Galleon in a commanding tone, "ya' was telling me about d' other Imps?"

Galleon looked around the table. He cleared his throat and began.

"Well, it seems that all the Imps, except the two of us that is, have all gone."

"Gone? Gone where? What on earth is ya' talking about."

"Banished. Possibly even killed."

"Killed? Killed by who?"

"By the Goat," Joshua said.

Lilly looked at Joshua and narrowed her eyes. "Is this da' same Goat that did away wit' all da' folks in da' Valley?"

"You heard about that?" Joshua asked. Lilly nodded.

"I think the Goat might be behind my father's disappearance too. That's why I'm here. I need to...well I...I need to meet with the Elder."

"Well, the Elder should be back any time now," Isabelle said. "Why do you need to see him, Joshua?"

Joshua shifted on his seat, deciding how best to answer. It created an awkward silence. Joshua cleared his throat.

"I...I believe the Elder can...um...help me," he stuttered.

"How? What do you need help with? And who is this Goat?" She turned to Sarah and squinted at her.

"Sarah, what's going on? What's this all about?"

Sarah's face reddened and she glanced at Joshua. There was another awkward silence as Isabelle stared at her. Sarah opened her mouth but before she could respond, a low-pitched horn sounded outside.

"Daddy!" she blurted out.

She stood up and ran to the front door. Everyone in the inn also got up and followed him out. There were so many people clamouring to see the Elder return, they couldn't all get out fast enough.

By the time Joshua managed to squeeze through, all he could see was the back of the Elder walking around the corner with a throng of villagers surrounding him. Sarah was at his side with her arm wrapped around him.

Joshua stood on tiptoes to try for a better look, but all he could see was Sarah and her father disappearing into a large hut across from the school. As soon as the Elder's hut door closed, the crowd disperse and people went back to their business.

Inside the Elder's hut, Sarah's father removed his bow and weapon belt. He laid the belt on a small table in the middle of the room and hung the bow on the wall over the fireplace, above a roll of cloth that lay on the mantel.

With his huge hands, he picked two of the logs piled neatly either on side of the fire and threw them into the flame. They ignited, creating a cloud of white, billowing smoke. Within seconds the smoke disappeared up the chimney and flames filled the fire pit.

The dancing orange flame was bright enough to light up the room, casting eerie shadows on the walls and up into the roof space. Numerous weapons adorned the walls.

On either side of the fire were two comfortable-looking chairs. The Elder sat in one of them. He looked at Sarah, who was still standing patiently by the door.

"Come, little one," the Elder said in a tender voice as he beckoned her over. "Come! Sit by the fire so I can see your face!"

Sarah beamed with delight. She walked over to the fire and sat in the chair opposite her father. The Elder took a deep breath, let out a sigh and smiled.

"I'm so glad you have returned to me, little one," he said nodding his head. Sarah's father was an imposing figure but for all his stature in the village, at this moment he was little more than a humble and proud parent.

"Tell me, little one, what did you find on your travels?"

Sarah's eyes peered up as she thought for a moment. She put her hands on her knees and rocked them side to side with a beaming smile.

"Well, I found so many new things, Daddy. I found lots of new types of food and found so many new plants and vines. I built traps and hunted for Wild Grassland Flarrets. They are so delicious. I never did catch a Wood-boar, but I did catch a Raetheon. It wasn't on purpose, mind you, it just sort of…"

Before Sarah could say any more, the Elder leaned forward with a smile and shook his head. Sarah stopped talking and looked puzzled. Her father chuckled to himself.

"I'm sure you have become a much more talented Fixer, Sarah. The skills you have learned will, I'm certain, serve you and your fellow villagers well, but that's not what I mean."

He leaned back in his chair again and tilted his head forward.

"You found something special whilst you were away, didn't you?"

Sarah squinted into nothingness and tried to think what it was her father was getting at.

He leaned forward again and whispered.

"Sarah," he said, shaking his head, "not something, someone."

Sarah's entire face lit up. She blushed and looked down at her hands in her lap. Since Sarah grew up without a mother, her father had done his utmost to care for and nurture her as best he could, but talking openly about matters of the heart was always something the two of them found awkward. The subject had rarely come up before.

Sarah had always been independent as a child and not at all interested in boys or romance. In her father's eyes, his daughter left Jemarrah as a girl to find new skills. He could see she had found much more and had returned a confident young woman.

"Whatever happened to the little girl that used to bounce on my knee? You've come such a long way, little one. I'm so proud of what you've become. Your mother would be proud to see you now."

Sarah smiled and shook her head. "Daddy, I'm not a little girl any more."

The Elder nodded and heaved a sigh.

"My little girl has grown into a beautiful woman. When did that happen, hmmm? So, tell me about him!"

Sarah took a deep breath and smiled. Looking away, she hesitated.

"Do you love him?"

Sarah nodded and her lower lip started quivering.

"Is he good to you?" She nodded again, and a tear welled in her eye. The Elder slowly nodded.

"Then that's really all that matters isn't it, little one?"

Sarah nodded and wiped a tear from her eye.

"I'd like you to meet him, Daddy."

"Soon, little one. I have some village business to tend to first. I will see him after last meal tonight."

Sarah nodded. She stood up and walked to the door. As she was about to leave, the Elder spoke.

"Sarah?"

With her hand on the half-open door, she turned and looked at her father.

He smiled. "It is good to see you again, little one."

She ran over and hugged him, tears of joy running down her face. The Elder held her for a few moments before kissing her gently on her forehead. She left the hut beaming, closing the door behind her.

Sarah made her way back to the inn where she found Joshua, Andrew and Galleon. Isabelle and Lilly had gone back to the school.

"I've spoken to my father! He wants to meet with you tonight!"

She threw her arms around Joshua. "He's going to love you. I'm just sure of it."

Suddenly, they heard a strange crying outside. It sounded like an injured animal but it was unlike anything they had heard before. They all went to see what the noise was.

"Blood-bats!" Galleon screamed. As they looked up, a hoard of the foul creatures flew towards them, weaving through the trees and making horrid ear-piercing shrieks. Two of them were tearing mercilessly at a Wood-boar tied to a table across the street. Dozens more of the bloodthirsty creatures streamed in, screeching from various directions.

Pandemonium reigned with everyone darting about trying to avoid the horrible beasts. Several Woodsmen launched arrows but the Blood-bats were too agile and easily managed to dodge them. They swooped so low that people had to duck to avoid their razor sharp talons.

Then, as quickly as they came, they flew off again into the forest canopy and disappeared. The people who had dived to the ground to take cover stood up and mumbled to each other in confusion.

The Goat paced furiously back and forth in His dark room. He roared with unrestrained rage.

"The boy has reached the northern village!" he screamed.

His eyes darted around the room as He thought frantically about his next move.

"He must not find the third orb!" He bellowed.

Elsewhere in the forest, Melachor was leaning against a tree, panting. Weakened from loss of blood, he struggled to remain standing. Filthy, bloodstained bandages clung to his infected wounds.

He took the mirror from his cloak and stared into it. His own hideously disfigured reflection swirled and the image of the Goat replaced it. The loathsome creature leaned forward and peered at Melachor. A malicious smile spread across His face.

"I understand," Melachor said in a barely perceptible voice. The Goat faded away and Melachor found himself again staring into his own eyes. He tucked the mirror back into his cloak, stood up and started running through the forest.

CHAPTER TWENTY-SEVEN
The Elder's Rage

After seeing the wave of Blood-bats, Joshua felt sure the Goat knew he was here in Jemarrah. Time was running out. He had to find the Orb of Suffering!

For the rest of the day they all waited at the inn. Joshua was feeling nervous about speaking to the Elder. He kept going over in his mind what he was going to say. Although the Oracle had told him the third orb was here and being guarded by the Elder, he still didn't know whether the Elder would let him have it.

"Would you relax, Joshua!" Sarah said. "You'll be fine."

Joshua paced back and forth. Just as he was going to say something, a low-pitched horn sounded outside. Joshua stopped and looked at Sarah.

"What does that mean?"

"The Council of Warriors has ended," Sarah said, with a huge grin. "Let's go."

"Good luck," Andrew said. Galleon nodded and patted Joshua's back.

Sarah and Joshua walked out into the cool night's air. Joshua noted several Warriors walking away from the Elder's hut, chatting to one another.

A billowing cloud of white smoke emanated from the chimney of the Elder's hut, and Joshua saw a flickering light coming from the windows. Sarah led her pride and joy to her father's hut and knocked on the door.

"Come in, little one," came the voice from inside.

Sarah opened the door and Joshua followed her in. The Elder was standing by the fire with his back to them. He tossed another log into the flame and a white puff of smoke erupted before the fire engulfed it and lit up the room some more. A bright orange flame filled the fire pit. The Elder stood back from it and looked into the flame for a second before taking his seat.

"Father," Sarah said, softly. "I want you to meet Joshua."

Sarah looked at Joshua, who wondered what he should do.

"Come and take a seat by the fire, young man!" The Elder spoke in a firm voice. Joshua looked nervously at Sarah. She nodded back at him with a smile. He walked over and stood by the empty chair.

"Please!" the Elder said as he gestured for Joshua to sit in it. Joshua did as he was asked. The Elder leaned forward and studied Joshua closely. His stare seemed to linger and Joshua felt uncomfortable. The Elder lowered his eyebrows.

"So, this is the young Woodsman that has stolen the heart of my little one?"

Joshua looked over his shoulder at Sarah. She smiled back at him and nodded. The Elder glanced over to see Sarah's nod of approval before catching Joshua's eye again. This was the boost to Joshua's confidence he needed.

"Um…I need to ask you something." Despite Sarah's reassurance, he still felt humbled by the stature of this imposing man sitting across from him. The Elder learned forward and squinted at the young Woodsman before him. Joshua wondered if the Elder recognised him, but he knew that wasn't possible.

"I'm looking for the Orb of Suffering. I've spoken with the Oracle. She said I could find the orb here with the Jemarrah Elder."

The Elder frowned and pursed his lips. "The orb is a sacred artefact. What do you want with it?"

"I need it to help me find my father. I believe he has been banished to another world by the Goat, and the Orb of Suffering will help me find him. The Goat is trying to kill me."

"Kill you?"

"Yes. He has already tried to the kill me once. He doesn't want me to find the orb."

The Elder's gaze shifted around the room. He then turned and locked his focus back on Joshua.

"Where are you from?"

"I'm from a village in the west, called Morelle."

"Morelle?" He repeated it several more times and looked into nothingness before sharply fixing his gaze back at Joshua again.

"Sarah's mother died at the hands of a Morelle Warrior!"

"I know. It was my father. It was an accident. He didn't mean to kill her."

The Elder sprang up and stared down at the nervous young man. Joshua pushed himself into the back of his chair.

"What makes you so certain of that?"

"I...I had an encounter...w...with the Orb of Time. I...I saw it happen. It was an accident. He...he didn't mean to..."

"ENOUGH! Enough of these lies!"

Joshua opened his mouth to speak but with the imposing figure towering over him he was lost for words.

"But father, please listen," Sarah cried.

"Enough, I said!" he snapped at her.

Pointing at Joshua, he shouted, "Get out! You dare come here and bring danger with you? Leave this place and never return!"

"Daddy, no, please!" Sarah frowned, standing her ground. The Elder just looked at her and both of them stood there eye to eye, neither of them backing down.

"You are to have nothing more to do with this boy! Nothing, do you hear me? NOTHING!"

Sarah bent over, crying. She collapsed onto her knees with her hands over her face and sobbed inconsolably.

Joshua's heart sank as Sarah looked up into the air and screamed with terrible anguish. Her eyes revealed a heart-broken torment that consumed her. Joshua looked on in horror. This was the scene he had seen play out when he first looked into the Mirror of Prophecy.

Sarah got up and ran out the door, still crying. Joshua glared at the Elder and ran after her.

CHAPTER TWENTY-EIGHT

Joshua's Pain

Joshua spent the next hour or more running through Jemarrah trying to find Sarah. He wanted to be with her and to comfort her but she was nowhere to be found. He tried the school, the inn, Isabelle's hut: everywhere he could think of.

Finally he slowed, then stopped. Sarah grew up here and if she didn't want to be found, there was nothing he could do.

His only option was to go back and confront the Elder. He thought if he could just explain everything, Sarah's father might be persuaded to see things differently. Over an hour had passed since the initial confrontation and Joshua hoped the Elder might by now have had a chance to cool off and reflect on what took place.

Joshua found his way back at the Elder's hut. Smoke was coming from the chimney and he could see flickers of light through the windows. He walked up to the door and knocked.

There was no answer. He knocked several more times, much harder.

"Who is it?" came the impatient voice from beyond the closed door. Joshua took a deep breath and mustered up as much courage as he could. His heart was pounding and he felt an anger welling deep inside. Joshua still needed the Orb of Suffering and although he had the greatest respect for the Elder, he was also feeling protective of Sarah and he wanted to resolve the conflict with her father for her sake.

"It's me, Joshua," he said with more confidence than before. "I need to speak to you. It's about Sarah."

There was a long pause. Joshua wondered whether the Elder heard him.

As he was about to knock again, the door swung open and the Elder stood before him. He looked furious.

"I have nothing to say to you."

Joshua stood his ground. "Look, your only daughter is out there who knows where, distraught because of you. Is that really what you want?"

Joshua felt his heart pumping. He could barely believe he had just spoken in that tone to a village Elder. He had never felt this angry or powerful before, but his instinct told him he must not back down.

The Elder looked at him for a few seconds before turning back into the hut. He didn't shut the door behind him, so Joshua followed him in. The Elder walked over to the fire and stood there gazing into the flames.

"Why did you have to come here? WHY?"

Joshua could sense real hurt in the Elder's voice. It was obvious he had loved Sarah's mother deeply and was hurting again now that those painful memories had been awakened. Joshua felt his own anger fade away.

"Look, I know you blame me for what happened all those years ago. I can only imagine how I would feel if our roles were reversed, but what's done is done, and there's nothing anyone can do about that now."

The Elder took a seat by the fire. He kept his gaze fixed on the flame and leaned his chin on his fist with his elbow on the armrest.

Joshua took a deep breath and felt himself calming down. Since the Elder was listening to him, he felt he had at least broken the ice. Joshua tried to imagine what was going through the Elder's mind.

"I lost a family member in those tribal feuds too. I had a sister who died at birth when Jemarrah marauders invaded Morelle years ago."

The Elder straightened up shifted his eyes in deep thought. He tapped the arm of his chair with his fingers.

"If everyone just went on hating each other, we'd all still be at war, even today." Joshua stared at him. "Is that really what you want? Is there no forgiveness in your heart? Not even for Sarah's sake?"

The Elder shifted in his seat and his lip quivered but continued to say nothing. Joshua sighed. His shoulders sank and he looked at the floor.

"Sarah and I love each other," he murmured. He noticed a tear welling up in the Elder's eye. "Isn't that the best that could come out of this situation? The alternative is for our people to continue to carry the hate."

The Elder turned and looked Joshua in the eye.

"You really love my daughter?" he asked, glaring at Joshua.

Joshua nodded.

"Do you love her enough…to let her go?"

Joshua pondered this question, confused. "L…let her…go?" he asked turning his head as if to deny what he heard the Elder say.

"I will give you the Orb of Suffering on one condition. You must renounce your love for my daughter, leave Jemarrah and never return to this place."

The two of them stared at each other. Joshua could sense the Elder was still in great pain. But then he then remembered the grave he had seen in the vision with Sarah's name on the tombstone. The thought had troubled him deeply ever since the orb experience and he had been hoping to find a way to prevent that tragedy. Could this be that opportunity?

He was deeply in love with Sarah, and the thought of not being with her was tearing him apart. He also knew he could never live with himself if something happened to her. Would she be safer if they were not together? Would being apart keep her out of harm's way?

The choice Sarah's father was offering him was heart-wrenching. He was being asked to give up Sarah in order to save her life. Just the thought of having to decide was agonising and Joshua felt raging grief rising inside at the thought that this might indeed be the only way to save her.

He felt overwhelmed. Joshua thought about what the Oracle had said to him back in the cave. 'The love you have found cannot last.' Was the Oracle's prediction coming true? Was this the inevitable moment the Oracle had foreseen?

By a cruel twist of fate, his intense love for Sarah would be the very thing that would now keep them apart.

"OK," Joshua whispered. He felt exhausted. His only consolation was the thought that Sarah would be out of harm's way. Perhaps she would live.

Joshua and the Magical Forest

CHAPTER TWENTY-NINE
The Portallas

As Joshua was coming to terms with his fate, he heard a creak behind him. He looked over his shoulder to see the door slowly open. There in the doorway stood Sarah.

Joshua could see dried tears below her reddened eyes. Her father stood up and took a deep breath. He stood there in silence, his chin raised and his lips pursed.

"Daddy?" Sarah pleaded.

Joshua felt heartbroken at seeing her like this, but the Elder remained motionless.

Joshua caught Sarah's eye. Although it tore him apart, he knew it had to come from him. Sarah needed to be convinced that he wished to end their relationship. Feeling numb on the inside, he spoke in a quiet, monotone.

"I'm sorry, Sarah. I have what I came for. It's for the best we end it here."

She burst into tears and Joshua's anguish soared as he summoned all his inner strength to keep from breaking down in front of her. He turned to the Elder and glared at him. Joshua felt a deep anger towards the man but needed to hide his feelings to remain convincing.

The Elder turned to the fire and took the roll of cloth from the mantel. After looking down at it for a few seconds, he held it out.

Joshua maintained his eye contact but his lip quivered as he reached out to take the third and final orb from the Elder.

He turned and walked over to where Sarah was still crying inconsolably. A brief glance at her was all he could muster as he desperately tried to shield his true feelings. Wondering whether this would be the last time he would see his beautiful Sarah again, he pushed the door open and walked out.

Joshua felt drained as he made his way back to the inn, where Andrew and Galleon were waiting for him outside. The sun had set and Jemarrah was now void of its earlier bustle. Smoke came from the buildings around the village centre and lights flickered from the windows. Everyone was settling in for the night and the hum of Dengles began filling the air.

"Where have you been all this time?" Andrew asked. Joshua didn't respond. He just stared down at his hands and the roll of cloth the Elder had just given him.

"Where's Sarah?" Galleon asked.

Joshua slowly lifted his head and stared into nothingness. He sighed with a vacant expression. "Sarah's gone. I had to let her go. It's the only way."

With the tears still drying on his cheeks and his eyes glazed over, Joshua knelt down. He laid the roll of cloth on the ground before him. His hands were shaking as he reached into his keeper bag and pulled out the other two orbs.

Andrew and Galleon watched over him as he carefully unwrapped each roll of cloth.

The three crystals glistening in the light of the rising moon. Their sheer beauty captured his mind. He slowly reached for the orbs.

There was a swish, and Andrew flinched as an arrow came out of nowhere and drove into his leg. He fell to the ground, screaming in agony.

Galleon looked around frantically but there was a second swish as he, too, was struck by an arrow. It penetrated deep into in his shoulder, and he also dropped to the ground in searing pain.

Joshua looked up to see Melachor approaching. His bow was pulled back to his cheek, the arrow pointed straight at Joshua's head. Blood dripped from the tips of Melachor's fingers as they strained to hold the tension of the bow. Joshua could see pain written across the desperate man's disfigured face. Melachor stopped just close enough for Joshua to see the whites of his eyes.

"Wait!" Joshua shouted. "I can save them! I can save your family. You don't have to do this, Melachor."

With sweat dripping from his face, the desperate man hesitated, trying to make sense of Joshua's words.

"You don't understand," Melachor cried. His arms strained under the tension of the bowstring. The arrow was pointing at Joshua's face, poised to shoot.

"He has them," he shouted. "He'll kill them unless I kill you."

Joshua sensed the torment in his voice. "Don't do it, Melachor!" Joshua shouted, shaking his head. "Listen to me! The Goat won't let your family go if you kill me. Think about it! He has no reason to. But if I open the Portallas, I can save them. They can come through the Portallas and into this world. Please, you must trust me. It's the only way."

Joshua reached his hand out towards Melachor. "Please, help me to open the Portallas. Together we can bring your family and everyone else the Goat has banished back into this world."

With the arrow poised to shoot and his arm shaking under the bowstring's tension, Melachor peered hopefully into Joshua's eyes. After a few tense seconds, Melachor slowly released the tension and lowered the bow to the ground. He shook his head.

"Please help them," he said collapsing to his knees. "Please bring them back."

Joshua bent down onto his knees again and looked at the three, glistening orbs, lying before him on the ground. He knew his friends were injured but he had to fulfil his destiny. Everything depended on it.

He picked up the Orb of Time. As he did so, loud screeching rang out and Blood-bats swooped in from different directions. Joshua remained calm and kept his focus on the Orb of Time in his hands. No matter what, he had to keep his concentration.

Andrew, Galleon and Melachor surveyed the skies as Blood-bats were flying at them from all directions. Despite their wounds, Joshua's two friends reached for their slingshots and began shooting at the foul creatures. Melachor joined them and launched his arrows into the air. The hideous screeching sounds pierced their ears, but they kept shooting.

Villagers came running out into the streets. Several armed Woodsmen joined them, and they too started firing at the Blood-bats darting between the buildings. With Melachor, Andrew and Galleon surrounding him, Joshua peered into the Orb of Time.

There was a flash of light and images formed and faded in his mind's eye. One moment he was looking up at his mother's face, and she was smiling down at him. He couldn't hear anything but she was saying something to him. The image blurred and was replaced by another of his sister's birth. His mother screamed in pain. That image lasted but a few moments before it was replaced with the image of Sarah's mother being stabbed by his father.

The images were appearing and disappearing so quickly that it left him no time to react. There was an image of himself looking out his bedroom window at a swarm of Dengles through the evening mist. The next moment, Andrew was jumping through that same bedroom window. That image blurred into another of his mother whispering into his ear, saying goodbye to him. He then saw Andrew running towards him through a cloud of vapour, before his first sight of Sarah in a makeshift camouflage suit flashed briefly into view. Joshua was reliving his entire life, but it was all happening in a split second and he barely had time to process each image as it flashed past.

The image of Sarah blurred and faded away. He was now floating, suspended in a blue flame in a cave. Echoes of the Oracle's voice rang through his mind and he could see Sarah screaming in pain before another blinding flash and the vision ended.

He looked down to see the Orb of Time drop to the ground between his knees. It was glowing and making a low-pitched hum.

Screeching Blood-bats continued to swoop in from all directions. Several had been speared by arrows from Melachor and the villagers but still more were arriving all the time and the air filled with the sounds of their high-pitched wailing. People all around were screaming with Blood-bats clawing at their heads and faces.

Joshua could make out the Elder launching arrows in quick succession at the bloodthirsty animals. Pandemonium reigned around him as the entire village battled the hordes of the Goat's foul creatures swooping through the trees.

Joshua scanned the throng of people and could see Sarah ducking as a Blood-bat swooped in and just missed her. He looked down and picked up the Orb of Suffering. In his mind's eye, all he could see was Sarah on her knees, screaming in terrible pain. Joshua's sorrow and grief gripped him as it had never done before and tears welled up in his eyes. His love for Sarah was absolute. He was overcome with so much sorrow, he felt it would kill him.

A tear dropped from his cheek onto the orb. It started glowing and humming in tune with the Orb of Time. Joshua put the Orb of Suffering down and picked up the third crystal, the Orb of Vision. As he did so, a Blood-bat came swooping towards him with its feet and claws thrust forward. It was just about to grab him with its razor-sharp talons when a Raetheon came diving in and collided with it side-on.

The two beasts clawed relentlessly at each other but the Raetheon somehow managed to gouge its claws into the Blood-bat's eyes. The wounded Blood-bat screeched in pain as the Elder launched an arrow straight through its heart. It keeled over and stopped moving. The Raetheon got up on its feet and morphed into the figure of a Woodsman. It was Protello.

"Quickly, Joshua!" the Metamorph shouted. "Activate the last orb! Open the Portallas!"

Joshua held the Orb of Vision to his face and peered into it. There was a swirling of clouds inside the sphere and a dark figure emerged.

Joshua was floating in a dark room. He felt disconnected from his body and an image of the Goat floated in front of him. Joshua could see the Goat's dark eyes glaring at him and felt the malevolent creature's unrestrained rage. The hideous creature's anger consumed him and Joshua again saw images flashing

243

through his mind. This time the images were evil. An image of Sarah being tortured flashed through his mind. She was being prodded with hot daggers and screamed in agony with Blood-bats hacking away at her face with their sharp claws. Joshua focussed his mind and tried to push the images to one side.

"It's too late." Joshua said in his mind. "Nothing you can do will hurt me now. You have helped me activate the third orb and now I can open the Portallas."

The Goat roared with anger and thrashed His head violently. His screams of outrage echoed in Joshua's mind. The rush of negative emotions tried to consume him. In desperation, he wrenched himself free from the link and the Goat's howling image faded.

He looked down at his hands and the Orb of Vision was glowing and humming with the others in unison. He put it on the ground and connected it with the other two. When the three orbs touched they began to pulsate with bright flashes of light. The humming sounds grew louder. There was a blinding flash, and a shockwave threw Joshua and the others across the ground.

A swirling vortex formed above the three pulsating orbs and a different world gleamed in sunlight on the other side. Joshua had done it; he had opened the Portallas.

Joshua and the Magical Forest

CHAPTER THIRTY
A Father's Sacrifice

The gateway darkened and became filled by an image of the Goat. The hideous creature was furious. Joshua watched as the hate-filled animal looked up into the air and howled. He then stared at Joshua and a hideous smile formed. It lasted briefly before the Goat's image faded. As it did, another wave of Blood-bats came flying through the trees, clawing at the villagers and tearing their flesh. People were screaming in agony and running around trying to escape from the bloodthirsty creatures of the underworld. Joshua turned to Galleon.

"Quickly," he screamed, "we need to summon those on the other side."

Galleon stood, clutching at his shoulder. With one glance at Joshua, he ran to the vortex, leapt in and disappeared.

Fresh waves of screeching Blood-bats streamed through the trees. There were hundreds of them flying in from everywhere, and they mauled the villagers mercilessly. Some people were trying to fight off two and even three of the demented creatures at the same time. Screams echoed in all directions.

Several villagers lay motionless on the ground with Blood-bats relentlessly tearing at their bodies and faces. Arrows flew in all directions as the Elder and the other villagers tried to knock the Blood-bats from the air. Several dozen Blood-bats had been struck and many more lay dead on the ground but new waves of fresh Blood-bats just kept coming.

Joshua looked at the vortex with wide eyes as people began jumping out in all directions, weapons aimed and launching. There was a mixture of imps and the other banished people from the Valley of Moross and they were firing their weapons repeatedly at the Blood-bats.

Swarms of arrows whizzed through the air every which way. More people streamed out of the vortex every second and they were all firing constantly. After several more minutes of mayhem, the piercing sound of the Blood-bats began to subside. One by one, the creatures of the underworld were shot from the sky until the dark forces of the Goat were vanquished and the last Blood-bat lay dead on the ground.

Joshua stood up and surveyed the battle scene. Hundreds of Blood-bats littered the ground. Several villagers had been killed in the onslaught. Many more were wounded. Some were being helped to their feet clutching at wounds.

Joshua stared at the vortex of the Portallas as a woman with two small children emerged. Melachor saw them and dropped his bow. He ran over and threw his arms around them, sobbing. Joshua felt a smile form across his face as he witnessed the tormented man reunited with his family at last.

With the dust settling, Joshua could see the Elder walking towards him with Sarah at his side. The Elder's hands and arms were stained with blood. Catching Joshua's eye, Sarah ran over and threw her arms around him. She held him tightly, crying. As she did this, a man came through the vortex.

Joshua's eyes widened and his mouth opened. It was his father. Joshua's father looked dazed for a moment as he took in the horrific scene of death all around him.

"DAD!" Joshua screamed at the top of his voice. His father turned and caught sight of Joshua with Sarah's arms still wrapped around him. He beamed at Joshua and walked towards them. As he got closer, the figure of the Goat appeared on the other side of the vortex again. He stared at all the Blood-bats that lay dead on the ground, then locked his gaze on Joshua.

Letting out an ear-piercing roar, He raised His arm and a golden arrow formed in mid-air. With a flash, the arrow hurtled towards Joshua and Sarah at a blistering speed. Joshua's father saw the arrow heading directly towards his son. He screamed and launched himself forward. The arrow struck him with full force in the chest and he fell. The Elder caught him before he hit the ground, the arrow impaled through his heart.

Joshua screamed and held his hands out as if to catch his father. Sarah looked over her shoulder at the sight of Joshua's father, limp in the arms of the Elder.

The figure of the Goat receded into the vortex.

Joshua ran over to his father and kneeled before him. "DAD!" he cried. The Elder looked down at Joshua's father. He put his finger against his neck to feel his pulse and shook his head.

As Joshua sobbed over his father's lifeless body, the Elder gently reached down and closed the dead man's eyes.

Joshua and the Magical Forest

CHAPTER THIRTY-ONE
Joshua's Destiny

Joshua was inconsolable and Sarah held him tightly. He had come so far and experienced such terrible pain. After an arduous journey, he had finally found his father but was unable to save his life.

Sarah's father held the limp body in his arms and got to his feet. He looked down at the dead man's face and a tear rolled down his cheeks.

"I know this face. This is the man who…"

The Elder met Joshua's eyes. He turned to the crowd and cried, "This brave man's sacrifice will not go in vain."

His lower lip quivered as he surveyed the dozens of bodies strewn across the ground in all directions. Tears rolled from his eyes. "None of those that died here today will be forgotten."

Nobody spoke as the Elder uttered those solemn words. The only sound was a few people sobbing. Joshua collapsed to his knees. He looked down at the three orbs on the ground. They were still pulsating gently, and he reached to pick them up.

As he did, there was a blinding flash, and he found himself engulfed within a blue flame. He levitated above the ground, disconnected from reality. The flame surrounding him wasn't moving. He was still aware of his surroundings but everything had stopped, and time itself was standing still once more. The Oracle spoke to him in a triumphant tone.

"Joshua, you have done well," the voice echoed. "You have fulfilled your destiny and helped my children return to this world."

Joshua's mind filled with a complex mixture of emotions, and he felt an anger welling inside him. He had gone through so much pain and had lost so much in the process. Not only had he found and then lost his father, but he also had to experience the grief at giving up his one true love. It was so unfair.

"Why?" he demanded. "Why did you tell me I had to give up my love for Sarah? Why was that necessary?"

Joshua felt that his sorrow would overwhelm him.

"My dear Joshua, you have experienced so much sadness in your young life, and your path has been a difficult one. For this I must ask your forgiveness. The power of the Orb of Suffering can only be summoned by one who has experienced true sorrow. I told you only what you needed to know to fulfil your destiny. My sweet Joshua, you have been through so much and done so well. The time for your suffering is now at an end. Go now and love her tenderly."

There was another bright flash of light and Joshua found himself kneeling on the ground with the three orbs before him. They were no longer glowing or making any noise. They were just three crystal spheres, glistening in the evening twilight.

Joshua stood up and looked into Sarah's watery, deep blue eyes. He threw his arms around her and held her tightly.

"I'll never leave you, Sarah," he whispered in her ear, "I love you so much."

He and Sarah embraced, their sobbing the only sound that could be heard.

Two Jemarrah Warriors took the body of Joshua's father from the Elder.

The Elder walked over to Joshua and Sarah. He stood before them and put his hands on Joshua's shoulders. He didn't say anything, but Joshua knew by this that he was no longer carrying any of the hate he had felt earlier. It was the seal of approval both Joshua and Sarah needed.

"There's one more thing we need to do," Joshua said to the Elder.

He looked at Melachor. "Do you still have the Mirror of Prophecy?"

Melachor pulled out the mirror from inside his cloak and handed it to him.

Joshua turned to the Elder.

"You need to be ready. There won't be much time."

"Joshua, no!" Sarah cried in horror. She held her hand to her mouth, shaking her head.

"There's nothing stopping the Goat from coming through the Portallas. I have to stop him. Otherwise, what was it all for?"

He looked at the Elder and nodded.

The Elder unsheathed his axe. He gripped its handle with both hands and gave Joshua a determined nod. Joshua lifted the mirror to his face. His image faded and a dark, swirling cloud replaced it.

The face of the Goat took form. The image cleared, and the Goat peered back through the mirror. The vile creature tilted His head forward and Joshua could see the whites beneath His malicious eyes. The Goat's face contorted with rage and He thrust His arm through the mirror and grabbed Joshua by the throat. His vice-like grip squeezed, and Joshua gasped for air, his legs dangling just above the ground.

The Elder raised the axe above his head and, in a single sweeping motion, slashed it down on the Goat's arm, severing it completely from His body. The sound of the Goat screaming in agonising pain could be heard fading into the distance. The mirror and the Goat's severed arm fell to the ground. The muscular limb lay there in a pool of its own blood, twitching.

After a few seconds, it stopped moving. Everyone watched in stunned silence as the arm crumpled into dust and was blown into the air and away through the trees. Now able to breathe again, Joshua picked up the mirror, but all he could see was his own reflection. The Goat was gone.

Epilogue

Several days later, the Elder stood in front of a large crowd that had gathered in the cemetery just outside the village of Jemarrah. A freshly dug mound of earth lay before him where Joshua's father had been laid to rest. Warriors and Woodsmen from all over Forestium were joined by Imps and people from the Valley of Moross to pay their final respects to those that had fallen during the battle. By the Elder's side were Joshua, Sarah, Andrew and Galleon.

"Today we honour all of those fallen in battle," the Elder told the crowd. "Those of you that are here today are here because of the courage, bravery and selflessness of a few."

Sarah took Joshua's hand and squeezed it.

"To find meaning in their deaths," the Elder said, looking directly at Joshua, "all of us must let go of the hate and learn to live with one another in peace and harmony."

He walked over to Joshua, stood in front of him and put one arm around his shoulder.

"And we must find forgiveness in our hearts," he said quietly to Joshua. The Elder smiled and walked away, followed by the crowd of people, leaving Joshua and Sarah standing, looking down at the grave.

Joshua shook his head sadly, "I'm sorry. I tried my best, but it wasn't good enough."

A single Woodsman was left standing in the distance after the crowd had gone. He morphed into a majestic Raetheon with huge, white wings and took to the sky. The Raetheon circled high above the site of the grave and cried three times before soaring off into the distance.

Several weeks later, Joshua and Sarah were walking hand in hand through the forest just outside of Morelle. Sarah looked at Joshua and giggled.

"You know you have mud down the side of your nose."

Joshua laughed back. He reached into his keeper bag and took out the Mirror of Prophecy. He looked into it to see what Sarah was talking about.

Joshua peered into the mirror. He opened his mouth and his eyes widened. Sarah's smile faded. "Joshua? What is it?"

He turned and stared at her in horror.

"The Goat. He's still alive. He has them. He has them all!"

THE END

Find out what happens to Joshua and his friends in the next instalment of the

Portallas series:

Joshua and the Magical Islands

Glossary

For full descriptions, visit
portallas.com

Andrew
Andrew was welcomed into the village of Morelle as an orphaned baby when he was just two years old. Both his parents were killed in an earlier skirmish during the tribal feuds that plagued the North and West back then.

Ashfer tree
Fast-growing tree prevalent throughout western Forestium.

Blood-bat
Dark creature of the underworld.

Bramock berry
Palm-sized berry from the Bramock bush. Bramock
berries are soft and green initially but turn hard and red
when ripe.

Bramock bush
Small bush that produces red berries and straight twigs.

Chirvel

Furry animal with bushy tail that lives in the treetop canopy.

Dengles

Flying insects that collectively hum whilst in flight.

Elder

Most villages of any significant size have an Elder - typically a former Warrior - that holds absolute responsibility for the village and its inhabitants. The Elder is responsible for all village matters, including deciding which Woodsmen will become Warriors, agreements with neighbouring villages, resolution of disputes, discipline, etc.

Fable

The son of a wealthy Trader, Fable inherited his father's fortune when he was a teenager and used it to set up an inn in the south of Forestium.

Finkle fly

Small, flying insect that comes out at dusk. Finkle flies don't make any noise but the tip of their tail can pulsate with a mild glow.

Fixer

Fixers build and repair things. Children with an aptitude for problem solving and ingenuity very often become Fixers. Most villages typically have dedicated Fixers but these skills may be applied more generally by Woodsman and Tenders in smaller villages.

Flarret

Wild Grassland Flarrets live on the open plains to the east of the River of Torrents and can also be found throughout the Valley of Moross.

Florelle

Florelle grew up in a small village in the south and was content to enjoy life as a village Tender when she met Fable.

Goat

A mystical and reclusive magical being, the Goat is the embodiment of evil and malevolence. His origins are unclear. Half-man and half-goat, he spends much of his effort jealously guarding against anyone discovering the power behind various magical artefacts hidden throughout the worlds connected by the Portallas.

Imp

Imps are a diminutive race of people that have traditionally lived in the Southern Tip, a peninsula in the far south of Forestium.

Innkeeper

Just about every village in Forestium contains at least one inn and there are numerous others on the various trails between villages.

Isabelle

Adopted as an orphan from a young age, Isabelle was taken in by the Jemarrah Elder after her parents and two older brothers were killed during a tribal feud.

Joshua

Joshua was born in Morelle in Forestium's far west. He is the firstborn child to Merinder and Sojath. Joshua grew up an only child but survives a sister that died during childbirth. Joshua's sister was not named and he was never made aware of her brief existence.

Lifren tree

Deciduous tree that grow sporadically throughout the west and north of Forestium.

Melachor

Formerly a successful Trader, Melachor now lives a reclusive life tucked away in a secluded hut deep within the forest in Northern Forestium.

Metamorph

Metamorphs are an enigmatic race of beings with magical powers. They can change shape to become other people or creatures and they have healing powers.

Mirror of Prophecy

Magical mirror - may be used to see briefly into the future. Also provides a means for the Goat to see and reach into Forestium.

Oracle of Forestium

An enigmatic being, the Oracle of Forestium takes the form of a small blue flame that levitates. Hidden deep inside a secluded cave in the Valley of Moross, the Oracle's location is difficult to find unaided.

Orb of Suffering

Magical orb–has the power to join with other orbs to open the Portallas when one has experienced true suffering.

Orb of Time

Magical orb–allows you to see events from your past or future.

Orb of Vision

Magical orb–allows you to commune with the Goat.

Protello

Protello is one of the few remaining Metamorphs living in Forestium.

Raetheon

Large, majestic, white bird. Raetheons flock in small groups and can be seen soaring high above and all throughout Forestium.

Razorfin

Fast-swimming, elongated fish with long snout and sharp teeth.

Sarah

Sarah is the only child of Serelle and Albert, now the Elder of Jemarrah. Although they have no other children of their own, Serelle and Albert took in an orphaned girl, Isabelle, when Sarah was very young and raised the adopted family member as their own. Sarah and Isabelle consider each other sisters and are very close.

Shrooms

Edible plant that grows prevalently on the ground and on trees throughout Forestium.

Tender

Tenders are the glue that hold villages together. They cook, clean and care for the other inhabitants of their village. Children that develop caring tendencies and a compassionate nature often gravitate towards becoming a village Tender. Approximately 4 out of every 5 Tenders is female.

Trader

As the name implies, Traders exchange and barter for goods and services between villages. Most villages have at least a single Trader but larger villages will have many.

Twiggling bush

A small bush with soft, edible leaves & roots.

Vines

There are various types of vine that grow voraciously all over Forestium.

Warrior

Warriors are the defenders of the village and responsible for the overall safety of its inhabitants. Woodsmen that are especially brave and/or fearless may become Warriors.

Wood-boar

Large free-roaming boar that lives on the forest floor and is found mainly in the West and South.

Wood-shire

Large horse-like creature.

Woodsman

The majority of boys in Forestium eventually grow up to become Woodsmen who provide for their villages by hunting. The most experienced and bravest Woodsmen may further develop to become Warriors, although there are fewer Warriors now that the tribal feuds are over.

Yucust-bees

Small bees that nest on the branches of a Yucust tree.

Yucust tree

Tall tree with horizontal branches. It grows throughout much of Forestium.

About the author

Christopher Morgan is a New York Times & USA Today bestselling author, blogger, IT Manager, graphics artist, businessman, volunteer and family man currently living in Melbourne, Australia. He spends much of his spare time volunteering for his local community. He creates visual learning resources for primary school children, which he markets through his company Bounce Learning Kids. He is also involved in local civics and sits on various community and council committees. When he isn't writing, Christopher visits schools to deliver presentations on writing and being an author.

Christopher was born in the UK and grew up in England's South East. At age twenty, he moved to The Netherlands, where he married Sandy, his wife of 30 years. Christopher quickly learned Dutch and the couple spent 8 years living in the far South of that country before they moved to Florida in 1996. After spending 7 years in Florida, Christopher and Sandy sold their home and spent the next 2 years backpacking around the world. Christopher has visited over 40 countries to date.

Whilst circumnavigating the globe, Christopher wrote extensively, churning out travel journals. He and Sandy settled back in the UK at the end of their world tour, where their two children were both born. In 2009, the family moved to Melbourne, Australia, where they now live.

Joshua and the Magical Forest is Christopher's debut novel and is the first in the *Portallas* series.

Other books by Christopher D. Morgan

Novels

Joshua and the Magical Forest - Portallas book 1

Joshua and the Magical Islands - Portallas book 2

Joshua and the Magical Temples - Portallas book 3

Joshua and the Magical Kingdoms - Portallas book 4

Short stories

Sarah's Farewell - A Portallas Short Story

Galleon's Prime - A Portallas Short Story

Andrew's Mission - A Portallas Short Story

Anthologies

Ever in the After: A charity anthology in support of the 2017 Lift4Autism campaign.

Dawn of Hope: A charity anthology in support of the Cajun Navy and their relief efforts for those affected by hurricanes Irma and Harvey.

80509294R00152

Made in the USA
Lexington, KY
03 February 2018